BURN FOR THE DRAGON

SOUTHERN DRAGONS BOOK 2

L.E. WILSON

EVERBLOOD
PUBLISHING

Deathless Night Series (The Vampires)

A Vampire Bewitched

A Vampire's Vengeance

A Vampire Possessed

A Vampire Betrayed

A Vampire's Submission

A Vampire's Choice

The Kincaid Werewolves (The Werewolves)

Lone Wolf's Claim

A Wolf's Honor

The Alpha's Redemption

A Wolf's Promise

A Wolf's Treasure (coming 2020)

The Alpha's Surrender (coming 2020)

Southern Dragons (Dragon Shifters & Vampires)

Dance for the Dragon

Burn for the Dragon

Mature and Desired (Seasoned Contemporary)

Be With Me

le@lewilsonauthor.com

Paperback Edition ISBN: 978-1-945499-55-5

Publication Date: June 3, 2021

Editor: Jinxie Gervasio @ jinxiesworld.com

Cover Design: Coffee and Characters

FOREWORD

This book was previously published with a different cover and the title, "Blood of the Master."

Dust clouds formed behind Everly's tires, quickly dispersing in the wind behind her as she pulled into the dirt parking lot of The Caves. It had been unusually dry the last few days, especially for spring, when Texans counted on a deluge of rain before the droughts of summer. But she was glad the temperature had warmed up a bit. At least for today.

She threw the car into park, and her eyes were drawn to the sky. Dusk was her favorite time of day, and the vibrant bands of pinks, blues, and oranges that made up a Texas sundown was a sight she'd never tire of. Everly sighed at the unfathomable beauty of it, and with some effort, refocused on the building in front of her. She'd never been to this particular club before. No one was allowed inside without an invitation. So, she'd come early, hoping to speak to the owners before customers started showing up. The place appeared empty. For now. But she knew as soon as it got dark, it would fill up fast with every lonely heart in a twenty-mile vicinity. Its notorious reputation was widespread, as were the rumors of the type of clientele they served.

Stalling for time to get her nerves under control, she flipped down the sunshade and checked her appearance in the little mirror, pulling her unruly hair forward to cover her ears. There was really nothing else to fix, as unlike most of the other women at the newsroom, she found anything but minimal makeup to be a waste of her time. She'd just sweat it off in the heat half the year or it would get washed off in the rain in the other. When her appearance was as good as it was gonna get, she closed her eyes and forced herself to take a few deep breaths. She'd been fighting for this assignment for months, ever since the night she'd walked outside of her house to do a little moon gazing…and saw the outline of a prehistoric creature flying across the sky.

Only now, she had an even bigger reason to come to this particular bar.

Her boss thought she'd lost her mind when she'd pitched the idea to him, but Everly knew there was a story behind what she'd seen that night. And she was ninety-six percent sure it had something to do with this club, and the mysterious people who owned it.

She was one hundred percent sure he'd finally given her the go ahead just to shut her the hell up and get her out of his office.

Everly grabbed her pen and notepad from the passenger

seat and got out of the car. It took her two tries to close the heavy door of the old, green Buick, due to the large dent near the front end (totally not her fault). Bending her knees and putting her full weight behind it, she finally managed to get it shut. Not bothering to lock a car no one would want to steal, she smoothed down her pencil skirt, plucked imaginary lint from the black cotton, and checked that her fitted blouse was tucked in and no buttons had come undone. Then she picked her way carefully over to the building, catching herself just in time to avoid a twisted ankle when her four-inch heel slipped on some gravel. She stared at the sign displaying the name of the club in large, bold letters across the solid steel door. No windows anywhere meant she couldn't try to peek inside before she went in.

Grabbing the door handle, she swung it open and marched into the air-conditioned, dimly lit interior. Although the sign outside said they didn't open for another twenty minutes, music already vibrated across the dance floor toward her, loud enough to rattle her teeth. She took a deep breath as her vision adjusted to the lack of light, and when she could focus, she found two pairs of male eyes watching her from the bar. A woman with hair nearly as wild as Everly's stood in front of them with her back to the rest of the club, but she turned with a ready smile on her gorgeous face when she noticed their diverted attention, her hand resting lightly—but possessively—on the knee of the man with the visible tattoos on his neck and hands.

Everly stayed where she was as a few words were exchanged between the two men, and then the non-tatted male got up from his stool and approached her. Well, at least he had none that she could see. She forced herself not to fidget as he strode forward with long, powerful strides, his sharp gaze never leaving her face. Dark hair fell forward to cover one eye as he passed under an air vent, and he pushed it back off his forehead with an impatient hand. The sides were buzzed close to his head. His face was perfect. Too perfect. Even under the short beard and moustache she could see that. Strong jaw. Lips just full enough to be deliciously kissable. Straight nose, but not too narrow. High-ish cheekbones. Deep, intense eyes under dark brows…

He stopped in front of her, just a little too close for comfort. Sensing his nearness for what it was—intimidation—she resisted the urge to step back. It was hard. From the time he'd gotten off his bar stool until this moment, he'd never broken eye contact, and if anyone asked her later, she knew she wouldn't be able to recall a single detail of what he was wearing. His lips moved, revealing a hint of straight, white teeth.

"Can I help you with something? We don't open for a few minutes yet."

She watched his mouth as he spoke, and it took her a few seconds for his question to penetrate the cloud of intoxication muddling her brain. He smelled unbelievably good, in a dark kind of way, and a jolt of surprise went through her when she had to fight the sudden urge to grab his arms and wrap him around her body like an obscene cloak.

Everly stuck out her hand a bit awkwardly. "My name is

Everly Taylor. I'm a writer at Capital Press. I'm doing a story on local businesses in the area and I was wondering if I could ask the owner a few questions."

His eyes narrowed the slightest bit as he studied her, and although her cheeks burned, Everly lifted her chin. She knew why he was looking at her like that, but she refused to let him cow her or make her feel she was less than just because she talked a little funny. She worked on her voice and her speech constantly, but on occasion, someone with a sharp ear caught her "accent" for what it was—a hearing impediment.

A few seconds later his expression cleared as under-standing dawned. However, rather than the pity she was used to seeing, she thought she saw a glint of respect in his dark eyes. He took her hand, his palm warm against hers, and shook it firmly, yet she had the strangest feeling he was handling her with kid gloves. "You can talk to me," he said. "My name is Hawke. May I get you something to drink?" He held her hand just a bit longer than was proper before he released it and motioned toward the bar behind him. "We have a wide selection of choices, including non-alcoholic if you prefer. Since you're on the job and all."

"I'll have a bourbon. Neat. Top shelf," she told him with wide, innocent, eyes.

If he was surprised by her request, he didn't show it. He indicated for her to precede him over to the bar where another man had joined the group. The new guy was nearly as good-looking as the first two—he reminded her of a young Richard Gere—but she saw right away that he lacked the animal magnetism of the other men. A magnetism that ol' Hawke here had in abundance, judging by the effect he was having on her respiratory system.

She joined the others at the bar and smiled hello but kept a professional distance. After brief introductions were made, Hawke stepped behind the bar and fixed her drink himself, sliding it across the smooth surface to her like a professional, then asked if she'd like to go into the office to talk, as they'd be opening the doors for business soon. Everly agreed and, drink in hand, followed him down the hallway to the left of the bar until they came to a locked door. Pulling a key from the front pocket of his slacks, he opened it and flicked on the lights before stepping back so she could enter first.

Everly walked into the room, taking in the barrenness of the décor. Other than an oversized desk, on which lay an unused legal pad with a pen perfectly aligned beside it, and a couple of chairs, the office was strangely devoid of any other furnishings. No file cabinets. No pictures on the walls. Nothing you would normally find in the office for a business.

She waited to see if he was going to sit behind the desk or make this a more casual thing by sitting in the leather chairs with her, but he chose neither. Instead, he shut them inside, leaned back against the door, and crossed his arms over his chest, blocking the only way out. Thick ropes of tight muscle in his arms tested the fine fabric of his mint-green, button-down shirt, and Everly felt the muscles low in her belly tighten in anticipation of feeling those muscles surging over her.

Logically, Everly knew she should feel threatened by his position and his posture. But she didn't. She didn't feel at all unsafe. It occurred to her that, perhaps, if the rumors were true, what she was feeling was exactly what he wanted her to feel. Yet, even that didn't change anything.

She raised her eyes to his face and he spoke. "So, Everly. May I call you Everly? What exactly do you want to know?"

Pinned by that penetrating stare once again, her heartbeat, so calm a few moments ago, picked up until she felt like the entire Kentucky derby was galloping through her bloodstream. She dropped her eyes to the small notepad in her hand, looking for inspiration within the swirls and lines of blue ink. When she found none, she stiffened her spine and pulled on her professional persona like a suit of armor. Glancing again at the questions she'd scribbled out right before she'd left the office, she asked the first one on her list, "Do you own this club?" Bracing herself for the impact of his intensity, she raised her eyes to his.

"I'm one of the owners, yes."

"Who is the other owner?"

He paused, but only very briefly. She wouldn't have caught it if she hadn't been so attuned to him. "My family owns this business."

"So, you and…" she pressed.

His head tilted to the side and one corner of his mouth turned up in the slightest hint of a smile at her perseverance. Everly could sense his impatience, though she couldn't see it by looking at him. "My father, recently deceased, opened the club fourteen years ago. Now it belongs to me and my brothers." He paused. "Would you like to know their names? Ages? Sexual preference? Blood types, perhaps?"

Ah. There it was. Even *she* couldn't miss the attitude in his questions.

He nodded at her notepad. "Don't you want to write this down? I'll wait."

Everly ignored his sarcasm and set to jotting down some notes. Then she gave herself an internal shake and plastered her best professional smile on her face. "I'm only trying to establish a baseline for my story."

Hawke pushed away from the door and approached her, not stopping until he was so close she could touch him if she so chose. She found herself staring at the smooth, tan skin at the base of his throat. He was doing it again. The crowding thing. But she refused to be intimidated by him.

Perhaps "intimidated" was the wrong word. "Overwhelmed" would be more apt.

He still didn't scare her, despite the fact he would be a good eight inches taller if she weren't wearing heels, and he had at least fifty pounds of pure muscle on her from what she could tell. As a matter of fact, the opposite was true. Everly was inexplicably drawn to him, and if anything, she wanted to get closer. He smelled like an alluring combination of dark spice and fresh rain, and she had the sudden urge to bury her face in the open "V" of his shirt and press her lips to the steady pulse she could see beating there. Heat emanated from his body, surrounding her with his warmth.

Something she found strange, though she couldn't put her finger as to why. But it was nothing compared to the blaze burning behind his eyes when she finally met them with her own, though the rest of his expression was carefully blank.

"What about you?" He lifted a red curl from her shoulder and rubbed it between his thumb and forefinger. "What's your story, Everly?"

"This isn't about me," she told him. At least, she thought she said it out loud. It was hard to concentrate on anything over the racing of her pulse and the heaviness in her loins.

His eyes dropped to her mouth for a brief moment before he locked his gaze on hers, and at that very moment she swore he could see right through her façade.

"Are you sure?"

Her blood chilled, cooling her ardor for this man she'd only just met. Surely, he couldn't know what she was really up to. Her boss didn't even know what she was really up to. "What do you mean?"

A smile teased the corners of his mouth, and he leaned down until those perfectly sculpted lips were less than an inch from hers. Everly held her ground, part of her—a very large part, she had to admit—wishing he would close the distance between them.

She wondered what it would feel like to be kissed by him. To be surrounded by all that heat and power pulsing from him in waves. To watch him become weak with lust. To see him lose control. To be the one who caused him to drop the rigid command he held over himself.

Her eyes closed, and her lips parted on a sharp inhale as

he leaned closer still. Warm lips, both soft and firm, skimmed over hers with a touch like a feather, only to leave her cold as he tucked his face into the side of her neck. His beard tickled her skin, making her shiver. But other than that involuntary movement and her harsh breathing, she found she couldn't move, couldn't react. She had the distinct feeling he was scenting her, like an animal did its prey, and she nearly burst out of her own skin when she felt his lips press against the pulse in her throat. Before she could comprehend or react to what was happening, the cool air from the air conditioner replaced the warmth against her throat, and Everly opened her eyes to find him once again blocking the door as if he'd never moved.

Except his appearance gave him away. The man she saw now both shocked and excited her, and she stepped toward him without realizing it, stopping obediently when he held up his hand. It was quite obvious now why it was strange to her that his body should radiate such warmth.

He was one of them. A supernatural creature living amongst humans like her. The rumors she'd heard were true! And her instinct to come to this hole in the wall bar had been right. And though she'd hoped to encounter one here, dreamed of it, she was in no way prepared for the reality.

Hawke's eyes burned, black as oil, and when he spoke, she saw the tips of what she could only describe as fangs. "You're going to walk out of this office and get in your car and leave. You won't speak to anyone on the way out. You're going to drive home. Tomorrow, you'll remember you weren't able to make it here tonight because you had to work late. You'll plan to come back tomorrow night. You won't remember me, this conversation, or anyone you met here tonight. Do you understand?"

Confused as to how he thought she could ever forget this night—or him—she nevertheless nodded. "I understand."

Hawke moved away from the door until he was standing before her. Lifting his hand, he brushed his fingers over her jawline and down her throat, smiling at the goose flesh he raised. "Goodbye, Everly." He leaned down until they were eye to eye. "You need to get out of here. Now."

He didn't actually speak the words. His mouth never moved, or if it did she didn't see it. Yet, she heard him in her head. He wasn't threatening her. He was warning her. Feeling like any moment she would wake up from a dream, she nodded. "Okay. Goodbye, Hawke."

He opened the door for her. She didn't hesitate but left as he'd told her to, walking out of the now crowded club and to her car. When she reached it, she gave the door a good yank, got in, and started the engine.

Heart racing like she'd just narrowly avoided a head on collision with an eighteen-wheeler, Everly hit the gas and got the hell out of there.

Hawke remained in the office for a good five minutes after the reporter left. It took him that long to repress the urge to follow her. Every cell in his body screamed at him to go after the persistent woman. And not for reasons that made any particular kind of sense. He'd never had such a strong reaction to a human before.

A woman.

It was fucking unsettling.

From the moment she'd walked in, fiery red hair curling in crazy corkscrews all over her head—in direct contrast to the tame appearance of her business attire—it was like someone had flicked a switch inside of him. She wasn't a beauty in the normal sense of the word. Her gray eyes were too bright and set a bit too far apart beneath dark brows that were refreshingly natural, not plucked into something that resembled the slash of a sharpie marker. Her nose had exactly three freckles across the top, easily noticeable against the fairness of her skin, and her bottom lip was slightly fuller than the upper.

It made him want to bite it.

And when she'd smiled, he'd noticed her two front teeth were longer than the rest, giving her a slight resemblance to a rabbit.

She was also deaf, or very nearly so.

Most people wouldn't have noticed. She must have worked hard to be able to speak as well as she did, cultivating her words and her voice, which only showed him how self-conscious she was that she was different.

Hawke pushed that aside. Her hearing or loss of had nothing to do with the wave of protectiveness that had washed over him, so strong he'd been momentarily lightheaded.

No, it wasn't a wave. It was more like a tsunami.

But her perceived weakness wasn't what drew Hawke to her. He'd met other women who had what they would consider a disability. Human women who had enthusiastically offered him their vein. None had brought out the reaction in him that Everly did.

No, it was something else. Something that brought out a side of him he'd never meant for her to see.

Which was why, against his better judgment, he'd told her to come back the following night. He would be better prepared tomorrow and would be able to control his baser urges. Or, perhaps it would be better to have Kohl or Andrew talk to the reporter and just avoid seeing her again altogether. He was too distracted by her. But it was good he'd told her to come back. That woman was up to something, and it wasn't a story for her little newspaper. No matter how sincere her words, the physical reactions of her body had given her away. To her credit, she'd quickly managed to control them, but it hadn't been quite fast enough.

Her thoughts, however, gave nothing away, because—astoundingly—he couldn't read them. Which only added to his curiosity.

Everly Taylor was a bit of a mystery. One he needed to solve before something happened that put the coven in danger. And he would start by checking her credentials at the newspaper.

The door opened, and Kohl poked his head in. "Everything okay?"

Hawke stared at his friend, unsure how to respond to that question.

Kohl stepped inside and closed the door, his brows lowered with concern. "What's going on?"

"I don't know." Feeling antsy under his friend's scrutiny, Hawke walked around the desk and sat down.

"What did that woman want? Everly? Is that her name?"

"Yes. Everly Taylor. She claims to be a writer at Capital Press."

"Isn't she?"

Rubbing the scruff on his face with both hands, Hawke sighed. "I don't know. I can't read her. I'll look her up and see what I can find out."

Kohl sank down into one of the chairs opposite him.

"How is that possible? I thought I was the only one you couldn't read."

"Until now, apparently." Hawke's mind spun, traveling back over hundreds of years in minutes, trying to recall any other time this had happened. But the truth was, it never had. Except for Kohl.

He'd always thought it was because his friend was a hybrid—half vampire, half dragon. But perhaps it was something else. It had to be. Kohl was the only one of his kind. Vampire-dragon matings were forbidden by both species. Kohl's birth had resulted in his dragon mother being banned from her Thunder and his vampire father abandoning them both. If it hadn't been for this coven of misfits that had taken them in, neither one of them would have survived. There was no way in hell there could be two like Kohl. It had to be something else.

"Is she a shifter?" Kohl was shaking his head before Hawke had a chance to answer the question. "Nah. She can't be. We would've known."

"She certainly didn't smell like any kind of wolf or other shifter local to the area." And Hawke had gotten close enough to get a really good whiff. Everly had smelled good enough to eat, that was for sure. Like sun-soaked peaches. Far from any kind of furry alternate personality. "In any case, I wiped her memory." He paused. "And told her to come back tomorrow."

"Why?"

Another question he didn't know how to answer. "I don't know."

Kohl was silent for a moment. He started to get up, then changed his mind and sat back down. Lines of worry creased his forehead as he said, "If you couldn't read her thoughts, how do you know you could influence them?"

The thought had crossed Hawke's mind, too. He pushed his hair back out of his face. "I don't. Not for sure. But she did exactly as I suggested when she left, so hopefully that won't be an issue."

"But you don't know for sure."

Hawke stood. He was tired of this conversation. "No. I don't know for sure."

THE FOLLOWING AFTERNOON, after a day of tossing and turning restlessly for hours on end until he finally gave up, Hawke hit the weight room for a few hours. Now he stood in his room, freshly showered and wearing nothing but a pair of black slacks and dress shoes. He stared at the five pastel-colored shirts on his bed, all button down, all long-sleeved. Fortuitously, the humidity level in the caverns was just enough to keep things wrinkle-free.

Picking up the pink and the purple, he turned around and held them under his chin one at a time, checking out his choices in the small mirror above his old chest of drawers. He'd had the ugly chunk of wood for two hundred years, but it was still in pretty good shape. Same with his bed, though he *had* updated the mattress over the years.

He chose purple. As he slid the shirt off its hanger and

shoved his arms through the sleeves, he ignored the little voice inside his head. The one that was laughing at him for worrying over his wardrobe like a female. It's not like he needed to go out of his way to impress the reporter. For one thing, he rarely needed to try to impress any woman. Most vampires didn't. And, at the risk of thinking way too much of himself, Hawke had always known he had a little something extra in the charisma department without even trying. To the point that he rarely showed his face in the club above ground once things really got going. It made for one too many confrontations with the other males in his coven when their human dinner guests caught an eyeful of Hawke and started second-guessing their choice of a date.

Secondly, it's wasn't like she was going to be sticking around very long. His sole purpose in having her come back again tonight was to do whatever he had to do to find out the real reason she was nosing around. Because he was about two hundred percent positive it wasn't for some little story about local businesses.

Hawke had made a few calls earlier that day, and her credentials checked out. Like any coven worth its salt, he and his brethren kept a finger on the pulse of everything that happened in the city they chose to make their home, including the entire area around it. They also had contacts throughout the country, mostly in other covens and even some shifter packs. The supernatural world may fight amongst themselves, but they worked together to stay under the radar and to keep things from turning into another, much bloodier, version of the Salem Witch hunts.

For the truth of the matter was, even though vampires and shifters were the superior species, humans far outnumbered them. If the overpopulated race ever decided to band together to take out the creatures roaming the night and threatening their children, the supernatural would lose. Eventually.

It was already beginning with Parasupe, the agency created by the human government here in Texas to control "rogue" vampires and other creatures. Only their version of "rogue" was anyone they ran across who wasn't human. Whispers of vampires and shifters disappearing under strange circumstances had been coming to his ears for a few years now. Nothing too close to home. Yet. But it was only a matter of time according to the info Kohl's female had brought them. And she would know. She used to work there, after all. And she was going to be one of the key players in taking Parasupe down.

Checking his appearance one last time, Hawke left his room and made his way through the underground caverns his coven called home. His path lit by subtle lighting the vampires had installed when the technology became available—because even they couldn't see in such complete and utter darkness; he forced himself not to appear overeager as he walked through the narrow tunnels. Water dripped in shiny rivulets down the smooth limestone, catching the light. Over the years, it would reshape the caverns as it had since the creation of the earth. But for now, it just added much needed moisture to the air.

Passing Kohl's area, he glanced down the narrow tunnel

that would eventually open into a small cave outside his room, more commonly known as the "foyer" between the two of them. Kohl wasn't there very often these days, as he and Devon preferred the privacy of the rooms beneath their favorite Irish restaurant while they waited for their house to be built. But Hawke would still look for him every time he walked by. They'd been friends and neighbors so long, it was a habit that was hard to break.

Nodding to a few male members of the coven just coming in, he came to the ramp that would take him above-ground. The reinforced door at the top took him straight into The Caves. Hawke breathed a sigh of relief as he left the confinement of the caverns and the door closed and locked behind him. Even after all the years he'd lived there, and even though, logically, he knew it was the safest place for them all in this piece of hell they called Texas, he still experienced a touch of claustrophobia underground.

The heavy beat of the latest dance mix blasted his ears, and through the fog of the smoke machines and the flash of the disco lights, he saw Andrew behind the bar setting things up for the rush of patrons who were no doubt in line just outside the door waiting to get in. Hawke checked his phone. They still had fifteen minutes before the club opened.

He took a deep breath, bracing himself for the rush of people, and froze. His gums burned as his fangs shot through in an instant, and a low growl reverberated deep in his suddenly parched throat.

Everly was already inside. He could smell her.

He spotted her in the middle of the dance floor with Devon and Frank—Devon's pain in the ass, but nonetheless amusing, ex-neighbor and friend. As he watched, Everly threw her head back and laughed at something Frank said while Devon shouted over the music, "What? What did you say?"

The ability to read lips appeared to be nearly as beneficial as having supernatural hearing.

As if she sensed his presence at that precise moment, her head whipped around in his direction, red curls flying. Tonight, she wore washed out jeans, a purple tank top, and gold Converse sneakers. A long, thin, gold chain hung around her neck, hanging nearly to her navel, and more gold glinted on her fingers. Her hair covered her ears, but Hawke would bet good money he'd find earrings to match if he could see them.

He hadn't noticed her penchant for shiny things the night before. But then again, he'd been caught unaware by the interesting mix of deceit and honesty in her clear, gray eyes, and by his own struggle not to throw her across the desk and sink his dick into her sweet heat while confessing all of his deepest and darkest secrets, just before he availed himself of her sweet blood. The same urge he was fighting now. The woman…did things to him. Unnatural things. And she did it seemingly without trying.

Hawke was determined to find out why.

Eyes locked on his, she raised her arms above her head and rolled her hips like a belly dancer, a smile teasing the corners of her mouth when he could do nothing but stare.

His upper lip twitched, baring the tip of one fang.

But he was saved from embarrassing himself when Devon finally noticed him standing there, staring like an idiot, and grabbed Everly's hand, breaking the strange connection. Waving to Frank to follow them, she pulled her over to Hawke. "Did I miss the memo?"

Hawke felt the tension leave his shoulders as he smiled close-mouthed at his best friend's female. "Hey, beautiful." Out of the corner of his eye, he saw Everly straighten at the compliment, a stab of jealousy shooting toward him. It seemed he wasn't the only affected one. The thought did not make him feel better. "What memo is that?"

"The memo that today we wear purple, of course." She grinned, specks of gold glinting in her brown eyes, looking between his dress shirt and Everly's tank top.

She and the reporter appeared to be hitting it off. The way women could bond on a dance floor never ceased to fascinate him. Assuming she didn't remember him, he allowed a look of mild curiosity to color his features as he asked, "Who's this?" Only then did he turn to acknowledge Everly.

Small lines appeared between the reporter's brows, and she looked up at him in confusion before her eyes dropped back to his mouth.

Hawke extended his hand. "My name is Hawke."

She looked down at his hand but didn't take it. "I know," she said. "I remember."

His heart beat hard within his chest, but only twice, before it settled into its natural rhythm. "You remember?"

"Yes. We met last night." She recovered quickly from her confusion, smiling at him. "I'm Everly Taylor, from Capital Press? You told me to come back tonight."

Frank spotted Andrew at the bar and excused himself with a loud, "Be right back, girls."

The fact that he included Hawke in this statement didn't elude the vampire, and he resisted the urge to roll his eyes.

Devon caught on, albeit a bit belatedly, and glanced pointedly at the reporter. "Should I not have let her in? I assumed it was okay. Hawke?" she prodded when he didn't respond right away.

Raising his voice so she would hear him over the music, he said, "No, it's fine. I just forgot for a minute. We had a busy night last night."

Devon gave him a strange look, and he willed her not to say anything else. She knew as well as he did that he never forgot anything.

"It's okay," he reassured her. "I'll deal with her."

She cast a worried glance between the two of them. "Okay. I'm gonna go join Frank at the bar. Make sure he's not harassing Andrew too much. Let me know if you need anything."

This last was directed at the reporter. Hawke found it amusing that Devon thought she could protect her from him if the need arose. Still, he hadn't meant to worry her. Tearing his eyes from the bewitching red head, he winked at Devon. "We'll be fine. Tell Kohl to come find me later."

"He's back at the house, making sure the downstairs is sun proof, and probably banging some nails himself. You know how he is. I needed to get away and came out for a girl's night. But I'll tell him if he makes it over." With a smile of reassurance at Everly, she wandered over to join Frank at the bar.

Hawke watched her leave, amazed at how well she was adapting to her new life with Kohl, even after everything that had happened to her at the club the night they'd met. He turned back to Everly, and he found himself faced with one raised eyebrow, arms crossed over her chest. "You'll *deal* with me? Are you going to kick me out? I haven't done anything wrong."

"I'm not going to kick you out."

"Then how do you propose you're going to *deal* with me?"

He decided to throw some honesty her way. "I'm going to find out the real reason you're nosing around my club."

She caught it like a pro. Didn't even flinch. "What makes you think I have an ulterior motive?"

Mark, the bouncer, opened the front door and humans started flooding in. Hawke held out his hand. "Would you allow me to buy you dinner?" His performance last night proved he couldn't be trusted to have her alone in the office again, but they did need to talk someplace a little less crowded.

He thought for a moment she was going to refuse, but then she said, "Okay. But I'm driving, and I get to pick the restaurant." Ignoring his outstretched hand for the second time that night, she turned and walked toward the door.

He growled low in his throat. This woman had no fear.

It made him hard.

With a nod at Andrew, Hawke followed her out past the line of people clustering around the front door and to her car. Business was picking up as the temperature rose, which also meant women's outfits were getting scantier, but he barely glanced at the row of exposed flesh that normally would have been more than tempting.

This night, his eyes were glued to the graceful back, rounded ass, and shapely legs of the redhead strutting in front of him.

His attention—and his hard-on—diverted when they reached her car and she struggled to open the driver's side door. He saw the problem right away, in the form of a large dent toward the front. Immediately, he broke into a cold sweat as he wondered who or what had caused it and if she had been injured. With an internal shake, he composed himself. This woman, and any injuries she may or may not have had, was none of his concern. Brushing aside her hand with a "May I?", he grasped the door handle and pulled it open easily, holding the door for her. "You don't lock your car?"

"Don't really see the need. Do you?" Then she pulled her keys from her front pocket and slid into the driver's seat.

Hawke shut the door behind her and walked around the front of the car to get in on the passenger's side. Other than a few pens and notebooks thrown onto the backseat, the car was surprisingly clean.

"I hope barbecue is okay," she asked as she pulled out of the parking lot.

"Whatever you want is fine."

"You might regret saying that when you see how much I can eat." She smiled, but he knew she was dead serious.

"I can handle it." Far be it from him to deny her the sustenance that kept her curves in such fine form.

The restaurant she picked was a little hole in the wall right off highway I-35, just a little south of The Caves. After she parked, he bid her to wait while he hurried around to help her with her door. She allowed him to play the gentleman, but he had the distinct feeling she was laughing at him.

Hawke shut her car door and followed her inside. Tonight, he would find out why she was snooping around his club and do what he needed to do to contain her.

CHAPTER 3

Everly had picked this specific restaurant on purpose. It was one she frequented often, and she knew, or was at least familiar with, everyone who worked there. So, if she came up missing, there was a better chance they'd remember she was there and that she hadn't been alone.

But other than the fact that he made her want to offer her naked body laid out on a platter for him to devour like some sort of pagan sacrifice to a very old god, Hawke had given her no reason to fear being around him. Nervous as a teenager and sexually frustrated? Sure. Who wouldn't be around a man who took her breath away with one searing look from those hypnotic eyes of his? But she had yet to feel afraid. If anything, weirdly, she felt safer than she had in a long time.

Waving to the owner's son behind the counter, she led Hawke to her favorite corner booth. The place was small, only eight booths and a few tables in the middle, painted

University of Texas orange and decorated with stars and longhorns, and it smelled like roasting meat, barbecue sauce, and cornbread. Everly's stomach growled in anticipation.

Hawke raised one eyebrow. "Hungry?"

"Starving," Everly told him. She had no shame when it came to food.

The waitress appeared, the newish blonde one with the braces, and Everly looked at Hawke, wondering if he would let her order or be one of those douchebags who thought he needed to prove what a man he was by ordering for her. Which she would promptly shut down.

He didn't. Instead, he smiled and waved his hand at the empty tabletop as if to say, "Do your worst."

Shaking her head at the offer of a menu, she started rattling off her order, and had to resist the urge to laugh as his eyes widened more with every addition.

The waitress, however, who'd waited on Everly before, was not surprised in the least. Brows furrowed, she scribbled down the order.

"And a diet Coke, please," Everly finished.

Unfazed, the waitress turned to Hawke. "And for you?"

"I don't suppose you have vodka?"

"No," she said. "But we have just about any kind of beer you'd want on draft."

"I'll take a pale ale," he told her. "Whatever you have."

"Anything to eat?"

He shook his head and nodded at Everly. "I'll share with her."

The waitress barked out a short laugh. "You might want to order your own, mister."

He smiled back, though it didn't reach his eyes. "I'll share."

"Okay." She didn't sound convinced as she closed her notepad. "Be right back with those drinks."

Everly watched him as he scanned the restaurant, stopping at each possible exit as though committing the layout to memory. "Do you always drink so much?"

His eyebrows lifted in surprise. "I'm sorry?"

The waitress set their drinks on the table, and Everly thanked her with a smile before taking a sip of her soda. "Alcohol," she clarified. "Do you always drink alcohol? It's all I've ever seen you drink."

Hawke saluted her with his mug before taking a tentative sip of his beer, then a longer swallow. He set it back down on the table and wiped one corner of his mouth with his napkin. "Well, being that the only places you've seen me so far are at a bar and a restaurant, I'm not surprised. But no..." He appeared amused. "Alcohol is not the only thing I drink."

Well, that didn't work. He hadn't been drinking the night before, and she thought he would say so and prove her earlier point. But it looked like she was going to have to be blunt. "Why did you pretend not to remember me?"

This time, her question didn't seem to surprise him. "I wasn't pretending. I see a lot of people every night. It took me a minute."

He was lying. For one, she wasn't easy to forget. And she

wasn't saying that out of some misbegotten place of ego. It was mostly because of her crazy hair and her…hearing challenges. Though she wore hearing aids that were able to pick out certain low-pitched sounds, it still sounded like it was coming through a wall of water, or a wall. She tried to speak and act as normal as possible, but she knew people still noticed. "That's bullshit. Try again." Leaning forward, she took another sip of soda as she waited for him to come up with a better answer to her question.

Hawke's eyes dropped to her lips wrapped around the straw, then lower, lighting on her breasts for a half second before coming back up to her face. He tried another tactic, equally as false as the first. "Okay. I wasn't sure if *you* remembered *me*, and I didn't want you to feel embarrassed, so I introduced myself again. Why is that strange?"

Oh, he was smooth. "It's not strange. It's just more bullshit."

He sat forward so fast she reacted instinctively, sitting back to put as much distance between them as she could. Her breath rushed from her lungs, the air between them suddenly charged.

His eyes drove into her. Apparently, he was done being vague. "What do you want from me, Everly?"

"I…" What did she want from him? Answers? Yes. His help? Definitely. But was that all?

She wasn't sure.

Everly was saved from answering by the waitress bearing a heavy tray of food. As she set plate after plate of brisket, beans, corn, chicken, cornbread, and coleslaw on the table, her movements dispersed the waves of tension convoluting the air. Hawke gave her a tight smile and sat back, lifting his mug to his lips as he turned to gaze out the window as he waited for the waitress to leave.

It took Everly a few more seconds to recover. "Thank you," she told the waitress, her eyes dropping to the feast in front of her. Eventually the mouthwatering smell brought her back to the here and now and her rumbling stomach.

Hawke touched her hand to get her attention. "Surely you're not really going to eat all that?" he asked when she tore her eyes from the food.

So, she'd been right the night before. He'd figured her out already. Everly fought back a sigh. It normally took people a few times before they knew she couldn't hear. Most of the time she had to tell them. And once they knew, it always changed things. People treated her differently. Guys made lewd remarks when they thought she wasn't looking. Girls stopped including her. She hated it. But it was what it was. However, she didn't want this man to see her as weak in any way, shape, or form.

Everly searched his face, but she found none of that in his expression, and she sensed nothing different in the way he regarded her. Curling her fingers into a fist to try to disperse the tingling his touch had left, she wondered for a moment if he was right. His presence was making her lose her appetite. Not because he was abhorrent in any way. Quite the opposite. Just the touch of his fingers pushed all thoughts of food out of her head and made her hungry for something else altogether.

But the moment was brief as the aroma of the restaurant's famous sauce reached her nose and her mouth began to water. She shrugged and picked up a chicken thigh, sinking her teeth into the perfectly cooked meat. This place really had the best food around. It was a shame they didn't get more business, but then again, Everly wouldn't come here as often if they did. She didn't normally like crowds. They tended to disorient her, especially if she was by herself.

Hawke sipped his beer as she ate, the expression on his face one of mild amusement as she plowed through each and every plate, but Everly wasn't about to play the wilting female just because there was a big, strong, male around.

When she was finished, he ordered her another soda and himself another beer, then waited until the empty dishes were cleared before he finally spoke again. "I have to admit, I kind of thought you were ordering so much food just to drain me of cash, but I see I was wrong."

Everly leaned back in her seat and licked her fingers. "I wouldn't be so petty. I'm a mature woman, not some silly teenager."

"I'm beginning to see that about you." He made a show of glancing around the table, and even looked underneath before he cocked one eyebrow in disbelief. "What? No notebook?"

At this point, Everly saw no reason to skirt around the issue. "Not for this conversation, no. This one is completely off the record."

Lacing his fingers together on the table, he rested his

weight on his forearms. "So, again, what is it you want from me, Everly?"

She took a deep breath. When she'd gone to the club the night before, she wasn't sure she'd find what she needed. But after Hawke's little display in the office, she now knew her instincts had been right. Still, knowing that didn't calm her nerves. If anything, it made her more nervous to have to ask this of someone like him. "I need your help to break into Parasupe."

If he was surprised by her request, he didn't show it. "So, I was right when I said your little local business article was a ruse."

"Yes."

"Do you really work for the paper?"

"Yes."

"Does your boss know it's a ruse?"

"No."

"What makes you think I'd be willing, or able, to help you with something like that? Breaking into a place of business is illegal. Besides, what could they possibly have done to warrant such behavior? Parasupe is an environmental protection agency."

"I don't think people like you worry about such trivial things as laws."

He eyed her warily. "What do you mean, 'people like me'?"

She refused to squirm under his stare. "People who aren't really…" She looked around to make sure no one was within hearing range. Or lip-reading range, for that matter. "People."

His head tilted slightly to the side, a smile teasing the corners of his lips. "I'm not a people?"

Mimicking his posture, she put her arms on the table and leaned into them. His smell came to her, dark spice and fresh rain, and she inhaled it deep into her lungs. That alone was enough to bring heat to her abdomen and make her thighs clench and her breasts swell, aching to be touched. She wondered what it would be like to be wanted by a male such as him. Would he be as domineering in bed as he liked to be in life? Or would it be the one place he liked to give up control? She swallowed hard at the thought. "I think you know what I mean."

But he wasn't going to make it easy for her. "No, Everly. I'm afraid that I don't." He made a point to look at his watch. "And unless you've got something better to discuss than whether or not I'm actually a person, I really ought to be getting back."

His sudden coolness toward her had her second-guessing herself. Had she imagined the heat between them last night? The way he'd looked? The way he'd smelled her? Was it all in her head that his order for her to leave and forget about him was anything more than just that? An order?

Not him trying to alter her memories?

As she sat in perplexed silence, he slid out of the booth and pulled his wallet out of his back pocket. He threw some cash on the table. "Good luck with your article. I'm sorry I can't help you." His eyes slid over her face and hair, then he gave her a smile and turned to walk away.

It was strangely wistful, and Everly had the most dreadful feeling she'd never see him again.

She scrambled for a way to keep him there. "But, how will you get back to the club?" That may have come out louder than she'd meant it to, as the entire restaurant, and not just Hawke, stopped what they were doing and stared at her.

She lowered her voice. "How will you get back? I drove you here."

Again, with the amused twinkle in his eyes. "I'll manage." He started to leave again, but turned back to say, "Perhaps I'll see you at The Caves sometime. Good luck with…whatever it is you're after, Everly." Then he strode out the door and left her sitting there alone like she'd just been walked out on by the best blind date ever.

Everly sat back with a huff and tried to ignore the sympathetic looks she was getting from the wait staff and one other occupied table toward the front—with three younger women sitting at it. Finally, she told them all, "It's okay. It wasn't a date. Just trying to get some info for an article I'm writing." With relieved smiles and nods, they went back to their business.

Looking out the window, Everly watched Hawke stride across the parking lot. Her eyes narrowed when he didn't head to the sidewalk as one would expect or pull out his phone to call someone for a ride, but rather veered to the left, where the lot ended and some actually decent-sized trees and scrub brush encroached. Between one blink and the next he was gone.

Just a normal person, my ass.

She may be deaf, but her eyesight was better than most people's, as was her sense of smell. Perhaps to overcompensate for the loss of hearing. She also had a spot-on memory, and she could've kicked herself for allowing him to make her doubt herself. Now that he was gone, and she could think straight again, she knew she'd been right about what she'd seen. Both last night at the club and just now.

Hawke was no ordinary man.

CHAPTER 4

Three hours later, Hawke finally got the chance to speak to Kohl alone. Hunting him down at his lakeside property, he wandered through the construction site until he found him talking to the lead builder on the far side of the partially constructed house.

The reporter hadn't come back, and he was both happy he'd gotten his message across and impatient with himself for wasting the last three hours hanging around in the club watching the door for a glimpse of red curls. He had no idea what her beef was with a company like Parasupe, but their conversation had him on edge.

Kohl showed no sign of surprise when he appeared around a partially finished wall. Most likely he'd heard and smelled him long before Hawke was close enough for him to see. Waiting patiently off to the side while Kohl finished his conversation, he nodded politely to the human male as he walked away, rolling up the blue prints for the house.

"They probably hate you, you know. Making them work all night instead of during the day, just so you can be here all up in their business."

Kohl grinned. "I pay them very well to work all night. And he thinks I have a sun allergy. Plus, I even help out."

"I'm sure they love that, too." Hawke fought to keep from laughing, but there was no hope for the sarcasm he couldn't suppress.

Kohl gave him a withering look. "I just want this place done, and I want it done right. So Devon and I have a place of our own to call home. She doesn't say anything, but I know she feels uprooted right now, staying in the hideout under the restaurant. And besides"—he took off his hardhat and ran a hand through his short, dark hair before tossing it to the floor—"I feel like I'm putting Margaret and her family out having us there all the time."

"That's a crock of shit, and you know it. They love it when we're there. It gives them somebody to fuss over."

"Ha! The only one she fusses over is Devon. She has Margaret and her brother wrapped right around her finger. All of that Irish food is plumping her right up."

"Are you complaining?"

"Hell, no!" Kohl grinned at his friend. "I like a woman I can sink my fangs into."

Hawke started wandering away from the noise of the construction. "Speaking of Devon, I saw her at The Caves earlier."

Taking the hint, Kohl grabbed his water bottle and followed him across the newly shorn grass that would soon be the front yard. "Yeah. She and Frank are having a girls' night out."

"So, you hiss at me whenever I have the gall to pay her the slightest compliment, but that throwback Richard Gere wannabe can hump all over her on the dance floor and you don't care?"

"Exactly."

Hawke did laugh this time as they reached the water's edge. The night air was crisp and cool, with just a hint of the humidity that would soon come with summer. He glanced up at the moon where it hung just above the horizon. It was full enough to diminish the brightness of the stars, and there wasn't a cloud to be seen. Dropping his chin, he stared out at the ripples of moonlight playing across the surface of the water and got around to what was really bothering him. "That reporter came back tonight. She was dancing with them when I came up from the caverns. The redhead."

"Oh, yeah? How'd that go? Did you find out anything new?"

"She remembered me." He felt Kohl stiffen beside him. "She remembered everything from last night."

Kohl became very still. "How?"

With a slight shake of his head, Hawke said, "I don't know."

"I thought you wiped her memory."

"I thought I did, too."

Kohl was silent as he swapped his water bottle from hand to hand, his expression carefully blank. And Hawke knew exactly what he was thinking.

"She's not like you."

"Is it the same? When you try to read her," he clarified. "Is it the same?"

There was something about Kohl's makeup that blocked Hawke from getting anything except the occasional stray word or thought, and it was his belief he got that much because Kohl was only half dragon, and half vampire. Still, most of the time, Hawke was locked out.

With Everly, however, trying to access her mind was like slamming into one of the concrete walls that made up the bottom floor of Kohl's house. Or five. "No. It's not the same. It's a total block."

Kohl lifted his head, breathing in a sharp intake of night air through his nose. Hawke knew what he was going to ask before he asked it.

"Why can't she be like me?" He wouldn't look at Hawke, instead staring out over the water. But there was no mistaking the edge of vulnerability in his raspy voice.

Hawke had asked him once why he didn't go seek out others of his kind. Yes, his mother had been banned for falling for the charms of a vampire, but she was long dead. Surely, the child she'd carried at the time wouldn't be judged so harshly. He hadn't asked to be born. And maybe, if he found the Thunder his mother had belonged to, he would still have family there who would help him learn to control the beast inside of him.

Kohl had just looked at him, confused, and told him he *was* his family.

"I didn't sense anything," he told him now. "She looks human. She smells human. And she has a hearing impairment. How would that be possible if she were at all like you?"

Kohl finally looked over at him. "I don't know. I don't know any others like me, except my mom. And she died before I could really learn anything useful about our kind."

But Hawke shook his head. It couldn't be. If there were others like Kohl on this continent, they would've heard about it before now. "It's not possible."

"Why not?" Kohl impaled him with a penetrating stare, daring him to come up with a better reason. His heart pounded within his chest, the sound loud to Hawke's ears. "I don't think it's such a crazy idea. We don't know every supernatural creature who lives on this continent. She could've moved here from somewhere else."

But Hawke wasn't convinced. "I would know if she was a shifter."

"Are you so sure about that? We weren't even sure about me until the first time it happened."

"That was different." Hawke knew he was being obstinate, but he couldn't help it. He didn't even know where the hell this attitude was coming from, or why.

Kohl stepped in front of him, blocking his view of the lake. He was slightly taller than Hawke, and the close proximity forced him to raise his chin to meet his eyes. Fire glowed behind the brown orbs. "We don't know anything about her, Hawke. Maybe that's why she's nosing around. Maybe she saw me flying around one night or something and is looking for others of her kind. Maybe she's without family, like I was."

Hawke shoved his hands in his front pockets and looked away with a shake of his head. "That's not the reason."

"Why are you being so stubborn about this? It's not a completely irrational idea."

"Why are you jumping to conclusions? You said yourself, we know nothing about her. Maybe she's just a nosy reporter who has no care for her own safety? Maybe she works for Parasupe. Maybe they're trying a different tactic to force one of us to do something they deem a punishable offense. Maybe…she's nothing but a trap." He decided not to mention that if that was the case they were all truly fucked, thanks to him and his uncontrollable urges. For now.

Kohl took a step back. "Do you think that's why she's really here?"

Grasping the back of his neck with both hands and looking up at the stars to ease the tension there, Hawke sighed heavily. "I don't know."

"Well, what did she say when you talked to her tonight?"

"She asked me to help her break into Parasupe."

"What? Why?"

"I don't know. I didn't stick around to get the details."

Hands on his hips, Kohl stared at the ground. "What do you think we should do?"

A short burst of laughter escaped Hawke before he could stop it. "What do I think? You're the coven leader now, Kohl. I came here to see what *you* wanted me to do about her." His gut twisted even as he said the words. If Kohl decided she was a threat, Hawke would be expected to handle said threat. It was what he did. It was what he'd done for hundreds of years for the previous Master. And he'd never had a problem carrying out whatever was decided. It wasn't his choice. He did what he was ordered to do, what he had to do, to protect his coven. And whatever the consequence…well, it wasn't on him.

Kohl shook his head and met Hawke's eyes. "I'm not the right one to make this decision. Hell, Hawke, I'm not the one who should be leading this coven. I'm not even a full-blooded vampire. It should be you, and you know it."

"You challenged the Master and won. *You* did that." He poked him in the center of his chest. "According to the laws, you are the new leader of our little family, and that's how it should be."

"But I'm not a full-blood—"

Hawke was growing weary of this argument. "It doesn't matter, Kohl. You won the challenge."

"No, the beast inside of me won the challenge."

"The coven has accepted you, Kohl. It's time you accepted it, also." He laid a heavy hand on Kohl's shoulder and caught his eyes with his own. "You just might surprise yourself."

Kohl sighed, lines of tension showing between his brows. "It's not right, Hawke. You're the elder now. You were the Master's right hand for too many years to count. You're way more prepared to take on this position than I am."

Slashing his hand through the air, Hawke fought not to growl at his friend. "You're wrong, and you know it. I'm not cut out to be a leader."

"I beg to differ, Hawke." He threw his arms out to the sides. "C'mon, man! You practically run this place."

"Under my Master's orders."

Kohl rolled his eyes, then he sighed. "What are you so afraid of?"

Hawke fought his rising temper. Turning away, he went back to stargazing. "I'm not afraid of anything, Kohl. You should know that by now."

"Hawke, you can't let one mistake fuck up the rest of your life."

"That one mistake was enough to make sure I don't 'fuck up' a whole lot of other lives. I don't intend to ever let it happen again."

"By letting others take responsibility for your actions?"

This time, he did growl. But Kohl only got more in his face. "Yeah, I get it. If you're carrying out someone else's orders, no one can put the blame on you when it all goes to shit. Especially not yourself. Your conscience will be clear."

"Fuck off, Kohl." But Hawke knew somewhere deep down that he was right. He was a coward. "I led them straight into a trap." He scrubbed his face with his hands. "I made a judgment call, and I was wrong."

"It was a mistake. A mistake you were lucky to survive."

"I survived because I'm a selfish bastard with a knack for self-preservation. Because I sent the others in first to make sure it was safe before I risked myself." Shame burned through him as he turned away, refusing to see the disgust that was surely all over Kohl's face. He'd never told anyone that part of the story before.

"I didn't know that."

Hawke crossed his arms over his chest to fill the sudden hollowness there. "Well, you do now."

Kohl was silent for a moment, then his heavy palm landed on Hawke's shoulder, much as Hawke had done to comfort him just a few minutes before. "That doesn't mean you wouldn't be a good leader now. We all fuck up. And we learn from it."

Oh, he'd learned plenty that night, and he remembered each and every moment of it. How could he not? The memories were seared into his brain.

Hawke inhaled some oxygen into his lungs to clear his head and changed the subject. "What do you want me to do about the reporter, Kohl?" His tone must have reflected how absolutely finished he was with all of this talk about him being the coven leader, for Kohl didn't argue with him anymore.

That, or his latest confession was enough to convince his longtime friend that Hawke was right to shy away from the responsibility.

"I don't know," Kohl responded. His brow furrowed, and he rubbed his hand over his bearded chin. "I'd like to find out more about her, and why she's so interested in us. Why she came to us for help, of all people." He grinned and slapped Hawke on the shoulder. "And I think you're the perfect one to do that, since she likes you and all."

A twinge of something raw and unfamiliar sparked within that hollow space inside of Hawke. He didn't trust himself to speak, so with a nod, he turned on his heel and got the hell out of there.

Everly felt a tap on her shoulder and looked up from her computer to see Tyson. He smiled and gave her a wink, then signed, "The boss is calling you."

Sure enough, Mr. Malone, the editor-in-chief of the paper, was standing at the front of the room, coffee in one hand and phone in the other. And if the red blotches on his face and neck were any indication, he wasn't happy.

Unconcerned—this show of excitement was more often than not caused by the possibility of a story and not by anyone in particular—she smiled at Ty, her closest ally at the paper, and grabbed her notebook and a pen before hustling over to her boss. She passed by row after row of empty desks on her way to his office, as most everyone else was out on some assignment or another. When she reached Mr. Malone, he threw his arms in the air, coffee sloshing onto the floor, then turned and stalked into his office as if to say, *What the hell took you so long?*

Everly followed, shutting the glass door behind her. "Sorry," she told him. "I didn't hear you."

He had the grace to look chagrined as he took his seat behind his massive desk. "I keep forgetting about…" He drew a circle in the air around his ear with the hand still holding his phone. "You've acclimated so well. I just forget."

"Um, thank you?" Sometimes, Everly wondered if her efforts to not let her disability *be* a disability harmed her rather than helped her. Skipping ahead to the most obvious reason she'd been called into his office, she started giving him a run down of what she'd learned so far. Which, since she wasn't about to admit what her real mission was with this story, wasn't much. He'd agreed to let her follow through on her suspicions with the condition that she didn't actually talk to anyone about it. Mr. Malone thought he was doing it to keep her from making a fool of herself. She knew he didn't really believe her. And she appreciated him trying to protect her career. Just as she was protecting him by lying to Hawke about her boss knowing what story she was really going after.

Flicking through her notes, she said, "I think I have a lead on my story. I've gone to The Caves twice now, that club just on the outside of town. The ownership records are kind of strange, and not just because they haven't been kept up. Quite the opposite. They've been meticulously kept, and the weird thing is—"

Her boss cut her off with a slash of his hand. "That's not why I called you in here. I'm sending you out on a new story. A real story. I just got word that the cops have someone holed up in a house six blocks away over in Sandy Hills. The guy ran into a house and is holding a couple of teenagers hostage. I want updates every quarter hour, and I want you to get in there and get all the statements you can. Find out who this guy is, his history, etcetera, etcetera."

Everly stared at him, her pen poised above her notepad. He was talking so fast it took her a minute to catch up. When he finally stopped and sat staring at her with his eyebrows raised high, she realized he was waiting for a response from her, and she cleared her throat. "Not to sound ungrateful or anything, but why not send Tyson? He's been dying to get out on a story like this, and I'm already working on the feature we agreed upon."

Mr. Malone rubbed his forehead, his arm blocking his mouth at times while he spoke. But Everly didn't have to read every word to know she wasn't going to like what he was saying, his body language told her everything she needed to know. When he looked up at her, his eyes begged her to understand.

But still, she had to be sure. "Mr. Malone?"

"Everly, I know you really believe there are things out there that go bump in the night. And I was willing to let you pursue it as long as you didn't have anything else to do and didn't piss anyone off too much. But now I've got a real story here for you." He smiled. "I'm giving you your shot at a real career here."

Her stomach dropped. "But, I thought you were on

board with this. I have evidence, Mr. Malone. When I spoke to you—"

"You thought you saw something in the sky, Everly. Something that looked like a…dragon, was it? And you thought you saw a vampire one night when you were walking home."

She did see a vampire. Three months ago, when her car was in the shop after someone T-boned her at an intersection and she had to use other means of transportation to get back and forth from the office. He'd run away when she came around the corner of the covered bus stop, a blur of color under the streetlights. No human could move that fast. And the man it had been feeding on had had two fresh puncture wounds on his neck and didn't remember a damn thing about where he'd gotten them. And yes, she'd seen something in the sky when she'd walked outside late one night to appreciate the beauty of the moon. And it wasn't a bird, or a plane, or anything else she could explain.

And, if she wasn't mistaken, she'd met a second vampire the night she met Hawke.

Mr. Malone laid his palm flat on his desk in front of her to get her attention. "Honey, this is your shot. You should take it. If you still want to pursue that other story when this is over or off hours, that's up to you." Leaning forward in his chair, he stuck his finger in her face. "But I need facts, Everly. Cold, hard facts. Photos. Audio. Video would be even better. I need proof that cannot be disproved before I let something like creatures who turn into bats at night grace the front page of my paper. Is that understood?"

Even without hearing the tone of his voice, she knew he thought this was all some crazy hoax, and yet a wave of relief washed over her. She could continue to investigate on her own, but having the paper backing her would give her a reason to be nosing around. "Yes. I understand."

"Great! Now get the hell out of here. And take Tyson with you. Oh, and Everly…"

She stood up and waited for him to finish.

"Don't let your fascination with all of this supernatural bullshit get in the way of the real story. Cops. Bad guy. Hostages. Now, go." Picking up the phone, he began to bark orders into the mouthpiece at some other poor soul.

Everly hustled back out to her desk, glad she'd grabbed her raincoat at the last minute when she'd ran out of her apartment that morning, because by the looks of the darkening sky, she was gonna need it. Her mind raced as she gathered what she needed and waited for Tyson to get his things.

"I'll drive." He signed the words even as he spoke them.

She rolled her eyes and signed, "Fine." Tyson had learned ASL shortly after they'd started working together three years ago. He'd never told her. He'd just shown up one day and started signing.

Caught off guard, Everly had been slightly embarrassed at first. She'd worked hard throughout her entire life to make her deafness a non-issue, learning to read lips and going to speech therapy. She wore hearing aids to amplify the few lower tones she could hear, and kept her hair long to cover them, though it made for more work for her to keep the crazy stuff somewhat tame. She'd learned to not only survive, but to do anything a hearing person could do.

Other than heed the warnings of car horns honking at her. Which was why Tyson insisted on driving.

Ten hours and forty-two minutes later, frustrated and tired, she pulled into her parking space in front of her apartment building and trudged up the stairs to her corner apartment. As soon as she locked her door behind her, she dropped her keys and her tote bag on the couch and kicked off her shoes, pushing the tops of her feet into the carpet one by one to ease the ache of wearing heels all day. Then she picked up her shoes and her bag and walked back to her bedroom. She didn't need to turn on any lights. Her apartment was on the end, and the soft illumination of the streetlights came in through her windows. And being that her place was basically one long room—the only door was on the bathroom in the back—they were sufficient so she wouldn't trip over anything.

Everly didn't mind the layout, or the intrusion of the lights. She liked being able to open her eyes at night and see all the way to her front door. Unless someone was hiding in her bathroom or the alcove of her tiny kitchen, she would see them. It wasn't much, but it helped her feel more secure.

She also had silent alarms that would vibrate and flash little red lights on the alert on her nightstand if anyone broke in through the front door or windows. One push of a panic button and the police would be notified to come check it out. She wasn't stupid.

Crawling up onto her bed, a cozy hodgepodge of mismatched pillows and colors like everything else in her place, Everly pulled out her laptop and sent a quick email to Mr. Malone, telling him she'd be in first thing in the morning with her story about the hostage situation. A few hours after she and Tyson had gotten there, the guy surrendered and came out of the house. They'd followed them down to the police station, along with every other reporter on the scene, to hear the official statement given by the police. Then they'd gone back to the neighborhood to try to find any eyewitnesses who could give her a better perspective on what had happened.

She'd lucked out and happened upon an elderly neighbor who'd been outside retrieving her trashcan when it had all gone down and had hung out to watch the drama unfold with one of her neighbors. They'd made a day of it with snacks and lemonade, like they were watching a reality show up close and personal, and the nice woman had made sure Everly had every detail she needed. Then that neighbor had gone and done one better. Her nephew happened to be one of the officers who'd responded to the call. And he was also single, don't you know. So, she'd called him up and talked him into coming back to talk to the "pretty newspaper girl". Lucky for Everly, he had a thing for redheads, and he'd been very obliging, telling her everything that happened along with a few small details the other reporters didn't get.

She should be thrilled she'd gotten a chance at such a

story. Even if she did have to fib a little and tell the young officer she had a boyfriend. But Everly felt anything but. Instead of feeling a sense of accomplishment with her career, she was distracted and restless. Her mind whirling with everything she'd found out about The Caves.

And about Hawke.

Which, she had to admit, wasn't much. Except that he was extremely good-looking, extremely confident in a hot, non-ego type of way, extremely sexy, extremely mysterious…

And extremely not human.

Human men didn't suddenly grow fangs or lose the whites of their eyes after smelling a girl. Or order them to forget any of that even happened while staring hard into their eyes and probing at their brain matter.

Oh, yeah. She'd felt it.

The first time, she'd thought she was just getting a headache. They'd been coming on more and more lately, starting out as nothing more than a nagging ache at the base of her skull and eventually spreading until her eyeballs throbbed with every heartbeat if she didn't catch it in time. Once the thing had gotten that intense, there was no treating it. She just had to deal until the pain went away on its own.

But when it happened again the second night she was with him, she'd realized that this was different. This was a gentle probing in the frontal lobe of her brain, kind of like someone was gently poking it. Overwhelmed with how good he'd smelled and her body's reaction to his nearness, she was unable to pinpoint what it was she'd felt until much later as she lay in bed, recalling everything that had happened. It was then she'd realized that what he'd really been trying to do was mess with her head.

And then there was the fact that he'd acted like he didn't remember her when she came back the second night, confirming her theory.

Everly glanced at the clock beside her bed. The Caves had been open for almost two hours now and was probably standing room only. Other than the rumors she'd heard, this was one of the reasons she had picked it as a possible hub of supernatural activity—why was that place always so busy? The club was nothing fancy. As a matter of fact, from the outside, it reminded her of an old shack some gold miner would've lived in, albeit bigger. And the inside was nothing special either, just the usual dive bar with a dance floor and a small stage where local bands sometimes played.

But, what it did have was lots of dark corners with private tables tucked away, an androgynous bartender who attracted both sexes and was generous with the alcohol, and regular patrons who were way too pretty and charismatic to be normal people in the middle of Texas. The door was carefully guarded, entry was by invite only, and it was always—no matter what night of the week it was—packed full.

The exhaustion she'd felt upon arriving home washed away as Everly rose and went to her closet to change into some clothes suitable to dance in. She'd go into the office early in the morning and get the article written for the day's feature.

Right now, she had to go try again to convince Hawke to join her cause.

CHAPTER 6

Hands linked behind his back, Hawke paced back and forth in the office of The Caves. The door was closed, protecting him from prying human eyes, but it didn't keep out the screeching of the vocalist on stage. Right at that moment, he hit a high note that grazed up Hawke's spine with razor-sharp fingers and ended on a shudder.

Scream metal was definitely not his type of music.

Normally, he would be far away from the club on a night like this, and he'd come aboveground with every intention of carrying out his duty to Kohl and the coven by hunting down the reporter and seeing what she was up to. Instead, he'd found himself pacing the office, listening for the sound of her footsteps, and scenting the odorous air of too many bodies pressed together in one place for the mere hint of the sweet smell of peaches warmed by the sun.

After a few hours of wearing a path in the old, wood floor and snapping at anyone who dared to interrupt his self-absorption, he realized he was waiting for Everly to come to him. Wanted to see if she would. And honestly, he was fucking disappointed that she seemed to have taken him at his word and given up on getting him to help her.

And, he had to admit, he was more than a little surprised. If anyone had asked him, he would've bet both arms that she was way more tenacious than that. But maybe not. Or perhaps she'd decided to stop wasting her time with him and go after Parasupe herself.

He was momentarily paralyzed at the thought.

Then he laughed at himself for overreacting. Everly was a smart woman. She wouldn't be so stupid.

Stupid, no. But stubborn? Persistent? Resolute?

Hawke rushed toward the door. His hand gripped the knob before he realized he'd moved. He had to find the reporter. If she tried to break into Parasupe alone, she would be killed. And they'd get away with it. Because she would be an intruder. And in Texas, you can shoot an intruder once they're on your property.

Actually, that law may have been changed sometime over the last century, but he doubted a company that broke the law on a regular basis would give a shit about whether they were within their rights or not.

He was so caught up in his thoughts, he actually jumped when a loud knock sounded on the door in front of him. By the heaviness of the impact of fist on wood, he'd guess it was Mark, the bouncer. And he wasn't alone.

Everly was there, less than a foot away from him with nothing but the office door between them. He knew she was there before he heard her voice, before the beat of her heart and the sweet scent of peaches leaked through the pores of the wood. He knew because more than any of that, he could *feel* her. Because her blood called to him in a way no other's ever had. It practically sang through her veins, begging him to taste, to drink, to possess.

With a sharp shake of his head, he fought down the urge to rip the door from its hinges and sink his aching fangs into her throat. Taking deep breaths through his open mouth, he compelled his body to calm down with a force of will he hadn't had to use in a very long time, until he was relatively certain he'd be able to control the blood lust.

His raging erection, however, he could do nothing about.

As he swung the door wide, he lost his breath once more. Everly stood beside Mark, tiny beside the vampire's overwhelming size, but not in the least bit intimidated. She grinned up at the bouncer as Hawke stepped aside to allow her to enter, and Mark gave her a saucy wink. With a nod and—was that a glint of a warning in his eyes, aimed at Hawke—he left her in Hawke's care and headed back to his post at the entrance.

Everly's scent made his mouth water. It burned down his throat to soak into his lungs before moving into his bloodstream until she filled his body and he knew nothing but her. Thirst nearly overwhelmed him again as the steady beat of her pulse filled his ears. He'd been stupid...*stupid*...to think he would be able to control himself around a creature like her.

However, her thoughts, as ever, were completely closed off as she brushed by him and bent over his desk to write something on the unused pad of paper lying on its surface. But Hawke wasn't really interested in what she was thinking at this particular point in time, not when that particular position stretched her faded jeans tight across her ass and her legs looked a mile long in the platform heels she was wearing. Hawke had the sudden urge to rip the denim away and press her flat onto the hard surface as he thrust into her wet warmth from behind.

The vision was so real he barely caught himself before moaning aloud. Things got no better when she straightened and turned toward him, the white T-shirt she was wearing so sheer it clearly showed the blue bra she wore underneath.

Dragging his eyes up to her face, Hawke didn't even bother trying to hide the physical evidence of what she did to him, and he was rewarded when her gaze dipped below his waistline and her lips parted on a sharp inhale. He would've laughed when her eyes flew back up to his face, gluing themselves there as if her life—or her virtue—depended on it, except he found nothing funny in the obsession he had for this woman. "What are you doing here, Everly?"

She stared at his mouth as he spoke, her pulse racing, heating her skin, the blood close to the surface now as it crept up her chest and into her cheeks, and he was never so glad she couldn't hear the guttural sound of his voice. She opened her mouth, but nothing came out, so she closed it again. This happened twice more until, finally, she said in a tiny voice, "I wanted to talk to you."

Hawke's upper lip twitched, his fangs swiftly descending as what little self-control he'd managed to maintain up until now completely fell apart. He found himself swiftly closing the distance between them.

Everly blinked hard a few times when he suddenly appeared directly in front of her, her lips parting on another sharp intake of breath. But to her credit, she didn't flinch or back away.

He knew he was being irresponsible, not bothering with the human façade he normally kept cloaked around himself at all times. Maybe he wanted her to see him as he truly was. Maybe he hoped it would finally scare her away for good.

Or, maybe he wanted to know if she would run from his "otherness" …or if she would be brave enough to embrace it. "What are you doing here, Everly?" he asked her again. He needed to hear her say it.

As though he'd wished the words from her lips, she told him, "I wanted to see you."

"Why?"

"I don't know."

"*Why?*"

He thought she would say it. Admit she wanted him as much as he wanted her. It wasn't as if he didn't already know what she was feeling. Her desire for him was made clear the moment he'd gotten close to her. But he wanted her to say it.

He *needed* her to say it.

Instead, she took a step back. "I came to ask you one more time to help me."

"Bullshit."

She blinked once. Twice. "What?"

Hawke closed the distance she had put between them. "I said, bullshit. You're lying. That's not why you're here."

"It is," she insisted. Those clear, gray eyes roved over his face, as though she was trying to memorize what he looked like.

But she didn't need to do that. Because Hawke realized, right at that very moment, that he had no intention of going anywhere. Jarred by the truth of his feelings for this woman he'd just met and barely knew, he forced himself to back off. He took two steps and stopped. "You need to leave, Everly."

She frowned, her chest rising and falling as she sucked at the air he'd put between them. "Hawke, please. Just hear me out."

"I'm not interested in your damsel in distress tale, and I'm not going anywhere near Parasupe." At least, not with her. The coven had its own plans for that "company." "And if you're smart, neither will you. So, unless you want to bend over that desk again—with a bare ass this time—you'll get the fuck out of here while you still can."

It was crude, what he'd just said to her. But for a heart-pounding minute, he thought she was going to take him up on his offer. Her eyes watched his mouth as he gave her the ultimatum, and though they widened a bit, he didn't miss the way the tip of her tongue wet her lips or how her hands balled into fists. She glanced at the desk, and the breath rushed from his lungs.

But then she pulled herself up, her spine ramrod straight. "I'm not sure who I thought you were, but obviously, I was dead wrong."

Hawke knew she wasn't talking about his vampirism, clearly on display at this point. Clenching his jaw to keep from apologizing to her for his insolence, he moved out of the way and allowed her to rush from the room.

He waited exactly three excruciating minutes, and then he followed her.

She'd left the club. He felt her absence down to his bones. But she hadn't gone far. Once he was outside, he moved swiftly to the shadows as he watched her fight to open her car door. Placing one foot on the back door for leverage, she gave it a furious yank before she finally got it open. She sat inside for a few seconds, staring at the door of the club with an unreadable look on her face. Then she cranked the engine, and backed up without looking where she was going, barely missing a pole. Gravel and dust flying out behind her, she took off out of the parking lot.

Hawke didn't need a vehicle to keep pace with her, not even with her lead foot on the gas. As soon as she got to the highway and turned south, the road opened up. Nothing halted his progress through the open fields alongside the road except for the occasional gas station or car dealership that lined the side of the highway until they hit the outskirts of San Antonio. After that, he stuck to the rooftops, easily leaping across the distance between them. It was late enough that most humans were ensconced in their homes for the night, and those that weren't wouldn't see him. He moved too fast for the human eye to see anything other than an occasional flash of his pink shirt, only stopping to confirm Everly's whereabouts when he was certain he wouldn't be seen.

Landing lightly on the roof of a two-story home, he crouched beside the chimney and watched her pull into the small, red brick apartment building across the street, parking directly in front of the stairs. It had twelve apartments—six on each floor. Everly got out of the car, not bothering to lock it after she got the door shut and made her way up the stairs and over to the top corner apartment on the left. There was a small round table on the walkway in the corner outside her front door, and she paused to pet a ragged orange tomcat lazing on top of it. She murmured something to the feline, then she unlocked her door and went inside.

Hawke heard the click of the lock.

With a quick glance around, he straightened and stepped down the incline to the edge of the roof. Crouching down again, he listened for any movement in or around the house he stood on, and when he heard nothing but the steady heartbeats of sleeping humans, he dropped to the ground. The cat watched him, tail swishing with interest as he walked across the street and approached Everly's car. Opening the door, he punched the dent out just enough to allow her to get in and out of her car without struggling so much. Then he popped the hood and did the same to the part of the dent affecting the seam of the door.

He didn't want to take the risk of someone seeing him climb the stairs, so he walked around the side of her apartments. Under the concealment of the large, leafy tree in the side yard, he scaled the side of her building to an open window that looked into her living room. The apartment was small, and from what he could see, cluttered with colorful furniture and tapestries that gave it a distinct bohemian feel. But it was clean and open.

To his right, he could see the front door, a small kitchen area directly in front of him, and an open hallway on his left. At the end of it, he could just see the foot of her bed. He heard running water, and after one last look—noting the security system this time—he dropped back down to the ground.

Happy to see she at least acknowledged the disadvantage of her hearing loss when it came to her safety, Hawke stared up at the bedroom window. He had no intention of ever invading her privacy or betraying her trust by going into her home without her knowledge or permission, but it was good to know he could get in if he had to. The security system would be easy for him to get around, and the fact that she was a renter was also good. All he had to do was find out who owned the building, and they could invite him in if an emergency arose.

Waving at the cat, who watched him with the bored nonchalance of a creature who couldn't be bothered but was still slightly curious, he went back to the club to get his car. If he hurried, he could get to Parasupe and snoop around a bit before the sun rose and he had to find shelter. He'd sworn to Kohl he wouldn't go all cowboy on the place after they'd shot up his club, but he needed to see what, or who, they had there that would make a smart woman like Everly want to risk her life by attempting to break into a place no human would be able to get into.

Fortunately, Hawke wasn't human.

Hawke called Kohl to let him know where he was. He didn't answer, so he left him a quick message telling him he was just doing a quick look at the layout and wouldn't be in any danger, and that he would check in before dawn, then he turned off his phone and stuck it into his back pocket.

Well aware his fondness for bright colors wasn't conducive to activities such as breaking and entering, he kept a black utility jacket in the back seat of his car—which was also black, with tinted windows—just in case, and he pulled it out and put it on.

He loathed the color, but sometimes there was no avoiding it.

Parasupe was located in the middle of Bumfuck Nowhere, Texas. Devon had given them the location, although she'd never been to this particular facility, so she couldn't give them more than that. The building she'd worked in was part of the façade put on for the general public, sixteen stories of modern architecture located in the heart of downtown Dallas, and when she'd tried to hack into the system, she'd found herself completely locked out. He knew she was working on that, but with Everly's plea for help, Hawke now had a new sense of urgency. And he was tired of waiting. So, he would just have to scope it out himself. He needed to know what was so damn important to her that she'd risk herself to get it back.

Leaving his car parked off the side of the road a few miles away, Hawke set out on foot. He expected the highest level of security, which meant there would most likely be cameras everywhere within a good two-mile radius. So, he kept low to the ground, moving fast and steady until he hit the perimeter, marked by a chain link fence at least fifteen feet high with rolls of barbed wire across the top. A bit overkill, considering he could feel waves of electricity rolling off it. The only one who would make it to the top—human or not—would be fucking Livewire from the DC Comics.

Or a vampire who could jump really high.

Cameras were at the top of every pole, the red pinpricks of their eyes easily spotted with his superior vision. Every few seconds, they would move silently on their necks, scanning the area before them. He counted the beats in between until he was certain their movements weren't random, then he moved. He began to skirt the perimeter, keeping low to the ground and staying out of sight of the eyes above him by using whatever he could as camouflage. Hawke kept his breathing slow and easy, refusing to give in to the serious case of *WTF are you doing?* that was threatening to overwhelm him. He could freak out later. Right now, he needed to stay out of sight, and get in and out without getting caught. If he could make it inside the main building without getting captured—or worse—he figured his odds of getting back out again were pretty good. But he didn't expect it to be easy. If that were the case, an army of supernatural creatures would've taken this place out months ago, as soon as it became clear this was not, actually, an environmental protection agency. Hawke could already see it would be near impossible for a large group to take the people there by surprise. But, perhaps, one lone vampire would have a better chance.

Three more barbed wire setups, two electric fences, numerous cameras, nine guards, and five infrared tripwires later, Hawke was outside the large center building with a stolen key badge in one hand and multiple dismembered body parts in the other. Not knowing what he would need from the lab guy who'd been stupid enough to work late tonight of all nights, Hawke had kept both of his hands in case he needed a fingerprint or palm read, and the head for the likely event of face recognition or a retina scan. He really hadn't planned on killing anyone, but the opportunity had presented itself, and Hawke had jumped on it. Quite literally. He'd take the body with him on his way out if he made it that far. If not, well, then the gig would be up, wouldn't it? A random dead body should come as no surprise.

The key badge got him inside a side door and into a vestibule barred by another door. This one needed a retina scan. Tucking the hands under his arm, he pried open the lab guy's eyelids and held the head in front of the scanner. With a green light and a soft click, he was in.

Hawke paused, listening for the sound of an alarm and letting his eyes adjust to the bright lighting. The first thing he did was look for the cameras, and he had to immediately tuck and roll around a corner to avoid being seen. Crouching on the floor in the shadow of a metal cart like they used in hospitals, he kept the severed limbs tucked against his jacket so blood wouldn't drip on the floor while he caught his breath.

That was too fucking close. He needed to be more careful.

Peering around the edge of the cart, he again watched the cameras. Unlike the ones outside, these appeared to be stationary, which was almost worse. At least if they scanned the halls, it would give him a little more room to move, depending on the timing. However, these would cover a larger area and overlap each other's viewing area.

Hawke retreated back to his hiding spot.

Fuck.

Chewing one corner of his bottom lip, he weighed his options, but not one of them ended with him getting out of there unscathed. Or, at all.

The bottom line was, it was too big of a risk. There was no doubt in Hawke's mind those camera feeds were moni-tored twenty-four seven. Like all vampires, he could move pretty damn fast, fast enough to be practically invisible on most feeds. But Parasupe would know that, wouldn't they, and they would adjust their system accordingly. One hint of something unusual on their feed, and all of those guards he'd left alive outside would be in here shooting at things they couldn't see until one hit him by a pure stroke of luck.

But he'd already gotten this far. He had to at least try, right? If he got caught, Kohl knew where he was. And unless they killed him immediately, there was a good chance Hawke would stay alive until reinforcements were sent to get him the hell out of there and away from these psychopaths.

So, fuck it.

Taking a deep breath, Hawke prayed whatever high school dropout was monitoring the feed would be jacking off to his latest fetish on his cell phone, and he began working his way down the labyrinth of hallways, keeping his head down and his face out of sight. He didn't pause anywhere long enough for the cameras to get a good look at him, but he didn't need to. As he made his way through the building and in and out of rooms, he easily memorized it all, and would be able to precisely recall everything to Kohl when he got back to the caverns. As there were no signs or other indicators of direction, he watched for anything that would help him know where he was in the stark white interior—a piece of gravel missed by a broom in the corner. A slight scratch in the paint on a corner of the wall. A discolored spot in the grout of the white floor tiles from a past spill. Hawke noticed and memorized it all.

He was nearly to the center of the building when he heard something that caught his interest. Veering immediately to the right, he took the next hallway.

No guards stopped him as he followed the sounds, and he soon found himself outside an unmarked door located at the end of a short hallway that seemed out of place. But he wasn't going to turn his nose up at the architect, for this way, he was out of sight of the cameras. The scanner was a fingerprint from the left hand, which was good because the limbs had lost all sense of warmth by this time. Hawke pressed the dead finger to the flat plate, and the lock clicked, allowing him access inside the room.

Hawke opened the door slowly, but there was no need for caution. A quick glance around proved there were no cameras in here, either. And no one was working late. Metal tables lined the walls, cluttered with microscopes and glass dishes and other odds and ends, except for the one just inside the door that held a large computer screen, mouse, and keyboard. The only lights were over what appeared to be a row of holding cells. But these weren't the kind you'd find at the local jail to keep the occasional drunk off the road.

They had bars, yeah. Titanium, if Hawke were to guess. But it seemed the bars were there only as a second resort to hold whatever they'd caught if it happened to get through the first layer of defense—walls of some type of glass, probably bulletproof and stronger than the stuff used to protect the heads of state.

There was a large cell dead center of the row, and it held

a prisoner. A man. He sat in the corner of the bare room, his nude form curled in on itself with his knees pulled up to his chest and his head resting on his folded arms. Lank, dark hair that looked as though it hadn't been washed in weeks fell forward to hide his face.

Releasing the door, Hawke let it swing closed behind him. At the sound of the soft click of the lock, the man raised his head to stare at Hawke. His bloodshot eyes touched on the dismembered parts tucked under Hawke's arm before sweeping back up to his face. There was no surprise there. He struggled to his feet, obviously weak and emaciated, yet still a formidable figure of a man.

Lean muscle covered his tall frame, and his sallow skin was covered in goose flesh. His hair was on the longer side, but it appeared to Hawke it was from the lack of a haircut rather than a sense of style as his jaw was also covered in an unkempt beard. The sharpness of his cheekbones and the unnatural thinness of his frame showed he was obviously being starved. But why? Who was this person? What threat did he impose on Parasupe? And, more importantly, how the fuck did Everly know him?

The male didn't bother to cover his nakedness but stood proud and defiant. "Who the fuck are you?" His voice was gravelly from lack of use.

Or, perhaps, from screaming for help.

Instead of answering, Hawke prowled the perimeter of the cell, looking for something that would tell him who this man was and/or why he was being held against his will. Seeing nothing of interest, he returned to the table near the doorway and the computer on its surface. It was still on, but it was in sleep mode and he had no idea what the password would be. He tried to override it, but his hacking skills weren't exactly up to par. He'd have to have Devon give it a shot remotely later.

"Hey! I'm talking to you, asshole."

Knowing there was nothing else he could do until they could get into that computer, Hawke picked up his spare body parts from where he'd set them down on the tabletop and wiped up the blood with his coat sleeve. Then, he turned to the prisoner, silently studying him for a moment. There was something about him. Something familiar. But he couldn't quite put his finger on what it was.

Without warning, the man rushed the glass, slamming into it face first with a scream of rage. And when he opened his eyes, they glowed, burning with a fire from within that Hawke was all too familiar with.

His own fire rose within him. A fire fed by jealousy and anger and disbelief.

This male was the reason Everly needed his help breaking in here. This male was the reason he saw that underlying sadness in her dancing gray eyes.

With a sob of frustration, the man backed away from the glass, covering his eyes with his hands. Hawke walked up to the bars. He needed to know. "I saw Everly tonight."

The man's head whipped up, his eyes panicked. "You stay the fuck away from her!" He rushed the glass again, moving faster than a human would ever be able to. For a split second, a shocked expression crossed his face as he looked at the cell like he'd never seen it before. Colors rippled up and down his arms, the skin loose, shifting on the muscle. The male didn't notice, or he was used to it. He focused on Hawke again. "You lay one fucking finger on her—"

"And you'll do what, exactly?" Hawke knew he was being a bastard, but he couldn't help it. Leaning forward, he pressed his forehead to the bars and stared through the glass. "I'll touch her any way and any time I want. Everly is *mine*." Then he flashed his fangs.

He expected the man to freak out and slam his face into the glass again, or at the very least let loose with a string of expletives. But, surprisingly, he did neither. Instead, he backed up a step, tears welling in his eyes even as he clenched his jaw in anger. He said nothing at all.

Remembering where he was, Hawke also stepped back. With a nod, he turned on his heel. He needed to get the hell out of this room. It made his skin crawl.

"Hey! Where are you going? Are you just gonna leave me here?"

Yes. Yes, I am.

Hawke didn't spare him another glance as he left the dragon shifter in the cell.

CHAPTER 8

Everly woke the next morning feeling like she hadn't slept at all. She'd tossed and turned all night, her body aching for something she couldn't give it. Occasionally, she'd find herself drifting off, only to wake with a start, sweating and feeling feverish. Other times she was so cold she couldn't stop shivering, longing for warmth all the blankets in her apartment couldn't give her.

After hours of lying there in this sort of twilight state, she rolled over and threw off her blankets. Forcing herself to get up, she got a quick shower, brushed her teeth, found some mismatched underwear, and pulled her wet hair back into a tight twist on the back of her head. In her makeshift closet, she found a simple blue-striped shirtdress and slid it over her head before going to get her phone where it was plugged in on her nightstand.

Her hearing aids stared at her from the glass dish she'd

put them in the night before. With a sigh, she put them in, then stared at her reflection in the mirror.

She pulled out some pieces of hair, enough so her ears were mostly covered. Then she scowled at her reflection. She looked ridiculous. Setting her jaw, she pinned most of it back again, only leaving a few strands so the devices weren't quite so noticeable.

It's not like she'd be seeing anyone she wanted to impress today.

A certain dark-haired, infuriating, sexy male entered her consciousness, and she firmly pushed him away again. She would most certainly not be seeing *that* person today. Or tonight. Or ever.

Throwing together a quick lunch, she slid on her favorite pair of Vans sneakers and a light black jacket before she rushed from her apartment. She needed to get into the office early so she could throw together the full story from the hostage situation yesterday for Mr. Malone. When she got to her car, she gripped the door handle and gave it a good tug, then almost fell on her ass when the heavy door opened rather easily.

"What the hell?"

She studied the exterior of her car. The dent was still there, but was it smaller this morning? Shallower, maybe? A blur of orange streaked across her peripheral vision and she looked up to find the old tomcat staring down at her from his superior height on the top of her car.

Everly squinted at the cat. "Did you fix my car?"

The feline sat down with a look that clearly stated he

thought himself above doing such menial labor, then turned his regal head to gaze off into the distance with his hunter's stare. He peeked back at her once, and when he saw she was still watching him, he turned his head away again with a swish of his tail, then began to wash his front paw.

Everly laughed and scratched him under the chin. "All right, big guy. You need to get down because I have to get to work." With a pat on his back end, she shooed him off the roof of her car and waited until he was in a safe spot on the stairs before she got in and started the engine.

The entire newsroom was empty when she arrived, so she switched on a few lights and got to work on her piece. When Mr. Malone arrived, she showed it to him, and he seemed happy with it. It was going on the front page of that day's paper. Everly thanked him and tried to be excited about the fact that her name was going to be on the front page, but her heart just wasn't in it. Besides, did anyone really read the paper anymore? Somehow, it just wasn't the same seeing your article on the home page of their website.

After the morning meeting, she spent the remainder of her day researching everything she could find about the Parasupe facilities. If Hawke wasn't going to help her, she would have to find another way to get inside herself.

The day passed swiftly, and before she knew it, Tyson was tapping her on the shoulder. Looking up from the computer, she realized most everyone had gone home for the day. She hadn't even eaten her lunch.

"Wanna go get a drink with us?" he asked her with a smile, signing the words as he spoke them.

Everly looked around at the empty room and raised one eyebrow.

Tyson laughed. "They're already at the bar across the street."

"Thanks," she told him. "But I need to get home."

He didn't believe her, she could tell from the look on his face, but he didn't press the issue. For that, Everly was grateful. No matter what he might be thinking, Tyson never argued with her when she claimed to be too busy to hang out after work, even though those days had gotten more and more frequent, and it was more than obvious she was being secretive.

"All right," he finally told her. "Next time. Be careful."

She noticed he didn't add "going home."

"I will."

With a casual wave, he sauntered out of the office, looking back once over his shoulder.

Everly smiled and waved, wondering—and not for the first time—if Tyson's interest in her was more than just as a coworker and a friend. Unfortunately for him, if it was, it was all one-sided. He was a good-looking guy, and she thought the world of him, but that thing that made a relationship more than just friends just wasn't there for her.

When he was gone, she sat back down at her computer and re-opened the page she'd minimized when he'd interrupted her. For the last few weeks, she'd been studying different types of security systems, and how to disconnect, break, or get past them. Kind of like Catherine Zeta-Jones in that movie where she was trying to capture Sean Connery.

Everly couldn't blame her. She'd chase after the handsome Scot, too, given half the chance.

But she wasn't stupid. This wasn't a movie. She knew she was taking her life in her hands just thinking about breaking into a place like Parasupe. The thing was, though, they were keeping someone there against his will. Someone she'd only just met, and yet cared about more than anyone else in the world. And she had no idea why they'd taken him, but she had this horrible feeling she was running out of time.

As someone who'd been in the news business a few years, she'd heard the rumors about that company. Rumors that said the whole "protecting the environment" thing was just a cover for what they really did. And those rumors went anywhere from running experiments on illegal immigrants to hunting down the things that went bump in the night. And like everyone else, Everly had taken those rumors with a grain of salt. Some of her more sensationalist colleagues had taken that bone and run with it, but as far as she knew nothing had ever been found to disprove the fact that Parasupe was exactly what they said they were, an environmental protection agency.

But then someone had broken into her brother's home and taken him while they were talking on the phone, and Everly had started to do some of her own digging. What she'd found had confused her more than ever.

A homeless person had seen her brother get forcibly

taken from his apartment. He'd also overheard them talking, things that would sound crazy to anyone else. But not to someone who would swear on her life she'd once interrupted a vampire's dinner and saw dragons flying in the sky. Everly knew if she was going to fight a company who hunted the paranormal, she would need someone of the same caliber on her side.

The Caves had been her first and only lead to someone who had a real chance of helping her. Or, preferably, multiple someones. Though walking into that place for the first time had secretly scared the hell out of her, meeting Hawke and seeing his reaction to her had given her real hope for the first time in weeks. His ardent interest was unexpected, but not unwelcome, especially if it gave her a better chance of talking him into taking on a place like Parasupe. But, attraction or no, it became quite clear last night he wouldn't be helping her.

Everly stared blankly at the screen. It had been unrealistic of her to think Hawke would do anything differently than what he was doing. He didn't know her. He had no skin in this game. What did he care about the fate of one human?

She couldn't go to the police about it. They would laugh her right out of the station. Why would a company who was all about protecting the environment kidnap someone? And if by some miracle she could talk them into going there and checking things out, by the time they went through all the red tape, she would bet her life Matthew wouldn't be there, and there wouldn't be a trace of his existence anywhere to be found.

She couldn't involve any of her friends, either. Not that she had many. She knew her neighbors well enough to say hi and wave, but they had their own lives, and so they rarely ran into each other. Plus, most people didn't seem to know how to handle her hearing impairment, and because she'd tried so hard not to make it a big deal, she'd never made the effort to really get involved in the deaf community. And she knew Tyson from work, but even though they heard crazier stories than this every day, she saw the way he rolled his eyes when he heard them. So, yeah. No. Sweet as he always was, she wouldn't be turning to him for any kind of support.

And that left her with only one option. She was just going to have to figure out how to get him out of there herself. Hence, her research on security systems. Also, over the past few weeks, she'd started picking up items here and there she thought she would need. A black beanie to hide her hair. Dark clothes and shoes. Tools. A lab coat if it came down to her going in on her own. But not all at the same time so it wouldn't look suspicious. She'd also rented a car under a false name for the drive up there tonight. Just in case she had to ditch it. One of her old sources had even hooked her up with fake identification and a security badge.

Everly was well aware that even with all of her careful planning, she would most likely end up sitting in a jail cell by the time the weekend was over. But it was a risk she had to take.

Taking a few minutes to erase her browser history, she shut down her computer, and gathered her things. Mr. Malone had just told her this afternoon that the leave she'd asked for had been approved. She'd told him she wanted a few days because her parents were coming to visit. Still riding the high of her inside scoop on the hostage article, he'd graciously told her she could as long as she "got her ass right back to work on Monday."

That gave her four days to get her brother out and somewhere safe.

Everly checked around her desk one last time to make sure she wasn't forgetting anything, knowing full well she might not make it back to report in the following week. On a whim, she jotted down a quick note for Tyson, and stuck it under a few things in her desk drawer.

She felt like she was walking on an electrified floor as she walked to the elevator. Every nerve in her body buzzing with anxiety. But she smiled serenely at the old white dude who got in on the fourth floor, and when they hit the bottom floor she told him to have a good night and walked at a steady pace out the foyer and next door to the parking garage.

Once she was in her old car, she took a steadying breath. *I can do this. Matthew is depending on me. There's no one else who will help him.*

She drove to a closed-down gas station and pulled around back. There, she changed into a pair of bootie shorts and a tight, black T-shirt with a deep "V" neckline. She left her Vans on. No one would be looking at her feet. Pulling a black bandana out of her bag, she tied her hair up doo rag style, making sure to tuck in any loose ends. Then she pulled out her rarely used makeup bag and layered it on. She topped off the look with dark, red lipstick.

Stuffing her work clothes into her bag, she locked up her car and left it behind the gas station. With any luck, she'd be back to get it before it was discovered and got towed. The car rental place was two blocks away.

If she received any catcalls for her disguise, she didn't hear them, but she did notice a few lewd stares. Perfect. Her plan was to hide right out in the open. She would be remembered dressed like this, but anyone who knew her at all would never connect the Everly they knew with this shameless woman strutting down the street with her ass hanging out of her shorts and her boobs on full display. She got her rental car without any hassle—a nondescript sedan —and drove back to her place to change again and pack.

She was going to Dallas. The location of Parasupe's headquarters and lab, and, hopefully, where they were holding Matthew.

The old tomcat was nowhere to be seen when Everly pulled into her apartments right as the sun was going down. Her heart fell. She'd been hoping to see him one more time before she left. Ah, well. He was probably off on a hot date somewhere.

When she got to the top of the stairs, she stood in front of her door digging around in her bag for her house key. She found it and stuck it into the lock, but before she had a chance to turn it, the hair rose on the back of her neck.

Everly froze, her skin crawling with the eerie feeling of being watched. Turning her head surreptitiously to each side, she checked the area around her. All of the neighbor's doors were closed. No one was about. Leaning over the railing to her left, she peered into the deepening shadows of the side yard. But she didn't see anything. Maybe it was just the cat watching her from his perch in one of the trees or something.

Or, perhaps, it was just her nerves. They were still buzzing as they had been since she left her office two hours ago. Everly turned the key in the lock, opened her door, set her bag and her keys on the couch, and turned, one hand reaching for the door to close it.

A man stood in her doorway, dressed in black, his face in shadows. Her first instinct was to scream, and she sucked in a breath, ready to bring the place down around her, but it lodged in her throat when he quickly stepped into the light.

Hawke's eyes traveled slowly down her body and back up again, pausing at her shorts and cleavage each trip. He didn't say anything, but he didn't have to. His stare wasn't condemning. Quite the opposite. It was completely shame-less as it caressed her heated skin with a bold touch that had her struggling not to rub her thighs together to ease the sudden ache between them. The tension in the air danced up her arms and legs, electricity that had nothing to do with her nerves.

His upper lip twitched, and Everly saw the points of his fangs when he spoke. "What the hell are you wearing?"

It took her a second to respond. "I always dress like this when I'm not working."

"Fuck no, you don't."

"How would you know?" And, really, what the hell did he care? Everly crossed her arms over her chest, a hand on each shoulder, blocking her boobs at least from his predatory stare, and pulled herself back down to reality. He'd completely blown her off last night. She didn't owe him any answers.

Her question got the reaction she was hoping for. The tension left his shoulders as he exhaled, but his fangs were still visible as he said, "I guess I don't."

"No, you don't." She turned her back on him and left him standing in the doorway as she went to the kitchen to get a glass of water, expecting him to follow.

He didn't. Instead, he leaned back against the railing, crossed his arms and ankles, and watched her through the open door with an unreadable expression.

Everly did her best to ignore him, but it was hard when she could feel his eyes on her, like a heavy fog, wrapping around the most intimate parts of her body. When she couldn't take it any longer, she faced him, keeping the kitchen counter between them as a barrier. "Is there something you want? Or are you just gonna lurk outside my door all night waiting for attention like the tomcat that hangs around here?"

One corner of his mouth lifted, and his eyes filled with mirth. "You didn't invite me in, Everly. And I would never presume to enter your home without an invitation. That would be rude."

Color her surprised. She assumed someone like Hawke would do pretty much whatever the hell he wanted. The buzzing of her nerves lessened to a hum. Maybe he was going to help her after all. Everly could've cried with relief. He was right. She wasn't this person. And it had nothing to do with her clothes. She wasn't brave. Or smart. Or...gutsy enough to break into a place like Parasupe and rescue someone like they did in the movies.

She needed his help, but to be honest, he scared her a little bit. Hawke wasn't human, she knew that. And though he'd never told her outright, she could easily guess what he actually was. And she had to admit, she felt a hell of a lot more ballsy when there was a dance floor or restaurant full of people around to keep him in check. "What are you, Hawke?"

This time it was his turn to look surprised. "What am I?"

Everly edged out from behind the counter and approached him warily. "I know you're not human, of course. That's the reason I came to see you. Well, it's why I came to the club. I assume there are more than one there like you."

He didn't confirm or deny her statement.

"And I've always believed there were others among us. Others like you. I've seen things. Things no one would believe if I told them. Well..." She gave him a small smile. "I guess you would."

"What kind of things?"

"I saw a vampire feeding at a bus stop one night." She chewed the inside of her cheek as she waited for his reaction.

Hawke tilted his head to the side, an expression of mild curiosity on his face. "And what did you do?"

She shrugged. "He ran off when he noticed me there, and I helped the victim."

"What else have you seen?"

"I walked outside to look up at the moon one night and saw…something. Flying in the sky."

No one else would have noticed it, but Everly often saw little details in people's body language that others didn't. Perhaps because her other senses were trying to make up for the missing one. So she noticed when his entire body tensed, though he didn't appear to move at all and his face gave nothing away. "What was it?"

She braced herself. "A dragon. Just like on Game of Thrones. I saw the distinct outline as it flew across the front of the moon."

The seconds ticked by as they stared at each other. Would she be in danger now for admitting she'd seen one of them before?

An even scarier thought came to her: was he here because he knew his little mind tricks didn't work on her?

"Perhaps it was a bird."

Nervousness momentarily forgotten, she snort-laughed. "It wasn't a bird."

Hawke uncrossed his arms and put his hands on either

side of his hips, gripping the railing. "And what do you know about vampires and dragons, Everly?"

"I know you are one of those things. And I think I know which one. I'm just not sure how the other comes into play." She held her breath.

He pushed off of the railing. "I think it's time you invite me in."

CHAPTER 9

"Are you going to hurt me?" The words were less than a whisper.

Hawke felt like she'd just stabbed him in the heart. "Of course not. I just think we need to continue talking inside, where listening ears won't hear us." Her heart was beating an uneven staccato, and he could smell her fear souring her natural sweet scent. He tried to lighten the mood. "And because I can't look at you anymore in that ridiculous outfit without thinking of Julia Roberts. Please, go change."

She glanced down at herself, running her hands over her stomach and hips like she'd forgotten what she was wearing. Hawke tried to swallow over the burning thirst in his throat. He'd totally lied just now. He loved what she was wearing, or rather, what she wasn't wearing. Her legs were strong and curvy and looked like they were a mile long in those shorts, and the tops of her exposed breasts begged him to sink his fangs into the soft flesh.

In all honesty, it was a nice distraction. Hawke was feeling a bit unsettled. He'd gotten out of Parasupe by the skin of his teeth. Leaving the dragon shifter in his cell, he'd gotten back outside without raising any alarms. Then, distracted by the male and who or what he was to Everly, he'd very nearly run smack into one of the guards. Changing direction from one breath to the next, he'd paused briefly to get his bearings and a camera had zeroed in on him, red light flashing in distress. Multiple walkie-talkies had all gone off at the same time, and he'd realized he was surrounded by guards, though they hadn't spotted him yet. A second later, sirens went off inside the building and he heard multiple pairs of boots running his way. Someone shouted orders. Keeping his head down and his face out of view, Hawke tossed the body parts and ran for his life.

When he reached his car, he drove south as far as he could and then pulled into a parking garage to wait out the day in the trunk. When he awoke, he'd come straight here. Sitting in the parking lot of Everly's building, he'd gotten on his phone and soon had a name for the owner of the apartments. Lucky for him, the couple lived just a few streets away. A quick visit and he had their invitation to enter any apartment he wanted.

However, he hadn't been lying when he'd told Everly he would never do that. Not only was it rude, it was an invasion of her privacy.

Everly raised her eyes to his.

"I'm not going to hurt you, Everly. I just want to talk."

She took a deep breath, the movement expanding her chest and pushing her breasts against her shirt. "Come on in."

Hawke stood frozen as he was. He'd heard her invitation, and even though he could've waltzed inside any damn time he'd wanted to, the sound of the words coming out of her mouth was the beginning of something he knew he wouldn't be able to stop. Because since the first moment he'd seen her, Hawke felt as though he'd been hurtling through space and time, arms and legs flailing, trying desperately to stop the momentum that had brought him to this exact moment.

This wondrous moment.

He stepped over the threshold and was immediately bombarded with the colors and smells and sounds of everything that was Everly.

"I'll be right back."

Hawke watched her walk to the back of her apartment, immensely relieved he had a few minutes to compose himself. He heard her rustling around in some drawers, then heard the click and lock of a door.

Something rubbed against his legs. Looking down, he saw the cat he'd met the previous night had followed him inside. Hawke picked up the feline and set him gently on the small, round table just outside the door. Then he went back inside and closed the door behind him.

While Everly was getting changed, he wandered around the small space, too jacked up to sit. A large, worn, L-shaped couch took up the entire wall left of the door. It was covered in so many blankets and pillows that it was impossible to tell what color the sofa's material was. But if Hawke had to guess, he would say something dull like gray or brown. Hence Everly's need to brighten it up with a rainbow of colored accents. To the right of the door across from the couch was a rickety stand with a small TV balanced on it. Through a cutout in the wall in front of him, he could see the kitchen, too small for more than one person at a time to make use of. Mismatched pots and pans hung from hooks in the ceiling above a counter covered in every type of modern cooking convenience being sold: a microwave, rice cooker, bread maker, and mixer. But the dishes were clean and neatly stacked in the drying rack and the stovetop was wiped clean. There was no dishwasher. There wasn't room.

Everly returned to find him fingering a tapestry of the moon and stars hanging beside the window. She had changed into a pair of blue lounge pants and held a fuzzy purple sweater closed over her chest. Her hair was down and most of the makeup had been scrubbed from her face. "So, let's talk."

To hide the fact that her current outfit did nothing at all to make it easier to be around her, Hawke glanced around the room until his eyes landed on the couch. "Would you like to sit?" Then he could've kicked himself. He was treating her like a guest in her own home. "I'm sorry. This is your—"

"Yeah." She went over to the smaller part of the "L" and

sat, tucking her hands between her knees as she waited expectantly for him to join her.

Taking off his jacket, Hawke folded it so the blood was on the inside and laid it across the arm. He chose a spot that wasn't too crowded with pillows and sat down gingerly. The couch was surprisingly comfortable. He leaned back, his muscles relaxing a bit, and rubbed his sweaty palms on his thighs. There was a good four feet between them, but she may as well be sitting on his lap for all the good it did. Hawke tried to focus on the reason he'd rushed over, but now that he was here, confronted with the realness of this woman, the steam appeared to have dispersed.

"Are you going to answer my question?"

Her question. What question had that been? Ah, yes. "Only if you answer one of mine."

She immediately agreed. "Deal."

"Who is the male, Everly?"

She visibly started, the color draining from her face. Her spine straightened, and she set her expression to one of mild curiosity. "What male?"

"The one they're holding at Parasupe." He decided not to reveal just yet that he knew what the male was. Perhaps she was aware of what he was. Perhaps she wasn't. He wasn't about to give away his hand before she told him one way or the other. "And before you decide what lie you're about to tell me, can I make the suggestion that you not. Please."

"He's no one—"

Pain lanced through his jaw, he ground his teeth together so hard. "Everly…"

She looked away, refusing to listen to anything more. But then she took a deep breath and turned back to him. "How do you know about him?"

"Because I went there last night after you left the club." He skipped the part of how he'd followed her home to make sure she wasn't going to do anything stupid. And, yes, to see where she lived. So, he could see she was safe.

"You went to Parasupe?" A tangle of emotions emanated from her—confusion, hope, but mostly fear.

Fear for him? Fear for the man being kept prisoner? Or fear for what he'd found out? "Yeah, I did."

She moved to the edge of the couch cushion, angling her body closer to Hawke. It might have been an unconscious gesture, but he felt it in every cell of his body. Her sweater fell open with her movement, and he noticed she wore a plain, white T-shirt or tank top beneath it. "You saw him?" She anchored herself to the couch with her hands, fists clenched so tightly on either side of her hips her knuckles were white.

Hawke took in her reaction with a feeling of unease. "Yeah. I saw him."

"He's alive? Is he okay?"

He shrugged, watching her carefully. "As well as can be expected." He paused, wondering how much to tell her. If it were someone he cared about, he would want every last detail. "He's being held naked in a cell like a lab rat and it appears they might be starving him. He's dirty and emaciated. And he's concerned about *you*."

Tears filled Everly's eyes, darkening the bright gray to

the chaos of storm clouds. She suddenly stood and paced away from the couch, keeping her back to him.

Hawke stood also. Without thinking, he laid a hand on the back of her arm.

Everly jumped and turned, startled eyes flying up to his face, and he felt a jolt of remorse for scaring her, even if it was accidental.

He held his hands up, palms out. "He's alive. But he's not in good shape. Mentally or physically." The blast of her sorrow hit him so hard, his knees nearly buckled from the force of it. "Who is he, Everly?" he demanded. "What is he to you?" Even as he spoke, he knew he had no right to the answers. He had no right to her at all.

But he wanted to. Desperately.

Everly pulled her sweater around herself and looked away, tight lines twisting the shape of her mouth.

Hawke's blood rushed through his veins as he reached out a shaking hand and gently clasped her chin, turning her face until she had no choice but to look at him. "Who. Is. He." He didn't want to know. Didn't want to hear her say it. But he *needed* to know. He could barely breathe as he waited for her answer.

Stormy eyes filled with pain rose up to meet his. "He's my brother."

Her brother. Not her lover.

His heart gave a hard thud in his chest, only to take off again as a surge of relief flooded his senses. Still holding her chin, Hawke drew her toward him and pressed his lips to hers. He didn't think about what he was doing or if he should be doing it. He was way past that. Emotions battled and tangled within him. Relief, sorrow, excitement, gratitude, rage, need, passion. His and hers combining into an overwhelming gale that battled the storm in her eyes.

Her brother.

Everly gripped his shoulders, the warmth of her hands seeping through the thin material of his shirt as he pressed her back over his arm, but she didn't push him away.

He released her chin and slid his hand into her fiery curls. *Soft. So soft.* Her lips. Her hair. Her breasts pressed against his chest. Soft and warm and all female.

Her scent swirled in the air around him. The rush of her blood filled his ears. She gasped for breath and he slid his tongue inside, denying her anything that wasn't a part of him. Her tongue touched his, tentatively at first, and then with more pressure until they were dueling for dominance of the kiss.

It wasn't enough.

Hawke tore his mouth from hers, fangs aching to pierce her flesh, throat burning with thirst, needing more. He rained kisses over her jaw and down her throat. One hand remained tangled in her hair as the other pressed her hips into his. He was so fucking hard. One fang skimmed along the tender layer of skin protecting the delicate veins of her throat.

A pulse of fear shot into him, crashing through the haze of lust, and without thinking he immediately stopped and straightened, pulling her up with him. He took her face between his hands and dropped his forehead to hers as he fought for control of the monster within him, his body screaming for blood and release. He should back away, put some distance between them, but he couldn't quite bring himself to let her go.

"I'm sorry," she whispered. "I just got a little overwhelmed. You're so…so…"

Hawke raised his head so she could see his words. Something he should have warned her about before things went this far. He knew she had her suspicions, but she didn't *know*. "Vampire. I'm a vampire, Everly. And right now I want you so badly I don't think I can stand to stay anywhere near you if you choose to deny me." No. He would have to leave if she didn't want this. It was the only way he'd be able to control himself. "But I *will* leave, if that's what you want."

"I don't want you to go." The words were frantic and taut with a mixture of chaotic emotions he could feel through to his bones. But her eyes were steady as they wandered over his face. His face that, right now, would scare most anyone else.

A low growl rumbled through the room and his upper lip rose in a semi-snarl, exposing his fangs, tasting her scent in the air.

Everly's eyes dropped to his mouth and widened. Her heartbeat sped up. And the blood…gods, the *blood*. It sang through her veins, a song warmed by his kiss and his touch, and flooded his senses until there was nothing else but her.

Everly.

CHAPTER 10

A vampire.

A vampire held her in his arms. Everly's heart pounded and she felt so lightheaded she didn't think she'd be able to stand without him holding her. But not from fear. Well, maybe just a smidge from fear. But it was more lust than anything else. "I don't want you to go," she repeated.

Hawke appeared to grow larger—harder—before her eyes. Muscles, already impressive, strained his shirtsleeves. His chest rose and fell with ragged breaths beneath her hands. And his olive-toned skin grew pale and pulled tight across the bones of his face. His upper lip lifted, baring fangs longer than she'd ever seen them. And the irises of his eyes, normally a dark brown anyway, deepened and expanded until they were nearly black. Yet they glowed with a vulnerable desperation and hunger. A hunger that echoed inside of her.

He was scary and exciting and breathtakingly beautiful.

"I don't want you to go," she told him again. An answering tremble ran through her when she felt him shudder beneath her hands. "And not because I'm trying to get you to help me." She felt it was important he knew that. "That has nothing to do with this. With what's happening now."

"I know," he told her. "I can feel your honesty."

It was hard to read what he was saying with his fangs in the way. Everly wasn't sure she'd understood him correctly. "You can feel me?"

He gave her a nod. "I can feel your emotions when they're strong enough."

"Can you feel everyone's emotions?"

"Not like this." He bent his head forward, his nose skimming the length of her throat.

Everly felt his chest rise and fall as he inhaled deep. His lips moved against her skin and words rumbled beneath her hands. Words she couldn't hear. And then he was kissing her again.

Hawke pulled her into him until her toes were barely touching the floor, and Everly kissed him back with everything in her. The twinge of fear she'd felt was gone. She didn't feel nervous. She didn't feel less than because of her disability.

She felt like she was home.

He shifted his hips and the hard length of him pressed against her stomach. Hugging her arms around his neck and lifting one leg, she wrapped it around his hip, positioning him against her core. Her body tightened and a shudder ran through her when he moved his hips again, hitting the exact spot she needed him, and she must've moaned aloud for he tightened his arms around her back and hips.

Everly had had a good number of lovers. Mostly in her younger, rebellious days while she was being transferred in and out of foster homes. But she'd never—ever—reacted like this to any of them. She'd been ready for this before he'd ever touched her, from the moment she saw him standing outside her apartment door.

He suddenly broke off the kiss and she sucked in a breath. Pushing her sweater from her shoulders, he kissed and nipped every inch of newly exposed skin. Vibrations tickled her nape. He was saying something. She shook her head with frustration. "I can't—"

The air cooled her skin, damp from his kisses, when he lifted his head so she could read what he was saying. "I want to see you, Everly."

Wordlessly, she nodded.

"I want to take you to bed."

Again, she nodded.

He didn't smile or have that look of satisfaction men got when they knew they'd succeeded in their conquest. Instead, time froze, the world fading around them as his eyes roved over her face, blinking in an expression of near disbelief. Sliding one hand down her arm, he lifted her hand to his mouth and pressed a reverent kiss to the pulse on the inside of her wrist.

Her breath caught in her throat.

The next thing she knew, they were in her room

standing beside her bed with its colorful patch quilt and mismatched pillows. She didn't even know how they'd gotten there.

Hawke gripped her hips, all of his focus on her. "Are you absolutely sure about this, Everly?"

He was giving her one last chance to back out. She touched his face with a steady hand, running her fingertips over the bones of his cheek and down to the edge of his mouth. She felt the harsh breath of his exhale stir her hair when they wandered too close to his fangs. And when she lingered there, his lips twisted into a snarl even as his eyes closed in bliss.

Fearlessly, she stretched up onto her toes and kissed him.

Hawke wrapped his arms around her and took her down to the bed, then rose up on his knees and pulled off his shirt, yanking it up and over his head without unbuttoning it. Tattoos covered his left arm and shoulder, dipping down to his left pec. Musical notes moved as his chest muscle moved, playing a song for the rose beside them. Timeless visions of people and places decorated his arm. Hard abs led to the "V" above his hips. She wanted to follow the curve of muscle with her tongue.

Everly started to sit up to take off her tank top, but he grabbed her hand and stopped her. She looked up to find him shaking his head. "I want to do it," he told her. "Let me do it." With excruciating slowness, he grasped the bottom edges and lifted it up and off, like he was unwrapping a gift.

Without taking his eyes from her, he tossed it onto the floor.

At his nod, she relaxed against the mattress, her breasts tingling, and her womb clenched with anticipation. But he surprised her again. Rather than joining her, he stayed as he was, touching her with nothing but his eyes for what seemed a very long time. She began to feel self-conscious, but then he reached out to touch her, his hand shaking as he ever-so-carefully caressed her breast. Everly closed her eyes, her back arching into his touch as he skimmed his palm over her aching nipple.

Something warm and wet touched the opposite nipple, and Everly gasped as his mouth closed around the rigid bud, sucking it into his mouth and flicking it with his tongue. Her hands found the muscles of his arms, tensed to keep him from crushing her with his weight. He moved to the other nipple, giving it the same attention, scraping the tip of his fangs over the sensitive skin as he released it. His hand between her hipbones pressed her into the bed and then went lower still, sliding between her thighs.

Everly cried out and bucked her hips. He'd barely touched her and her entire body was shaking with need. "Hawke, please." She had no idea if he'd heard her or if she'd even said the words aloud, but a moment later and her pajama pants were joining her shirt on the floor.

He touched her face and she opened her eyes to find Hawke hovering over her. Capturing her eyes with his and holding them, he silently commanded her to watch as he kissed his way down her stomach, nipping her here and there before soothing her with his tongue. When he reached her hipbone, he spread her thighs wide with his hands and lowered his head, burying his nose in the tight curls. His tongue touched her and hot pleasure shot through her womb.

Eyes still locked to hers, he smiled a devil's smile.

Everly nearly came from that smile alone as she let her head fall back with a moan. His mouth covered her, licking, sucking, bringing her right to the edge and then easing her gently down again. Somewhere between the waves of pleasure she wondered how he managed not to bite her with those fangs, but the wisp of thought was there and gone again, lost in the clenching of her muscles around the finger he pushed inside of her.

He didn't tease her. No. This was a full-on assault. The pressure built, waves of almost painful pleasure building one upon the other, faster and harder, and Everly gripped the quilt, powerless to stop it as she rode them higher and higher. Her body wasn't her own anymore. It was Hawke's to do with as he pleased, and she was powerless against his will.

The back of her neck burned. Her breasts swelled. And her nipples ached. Her breath came in pants. Every muscle strained, her body bowing uncontrollably, chasing that crest that would take her crashing down over the edge.

But she was unprepared for the intensity of it when it finally happened. With a flick of his tongue, he nipped her clit as he pressed another finger deep inside of her. Everly came with a breathless cry, her body convulsing even with the heavy arm he threw over her hips to hold her to his mouth.

And then the weight of his body was hot and heavy on top of her. Everly pulled him to her, still riding the waves of her orgasm, and cried out again when he slid balls deep inside of her with one thrust. His mouth covered hers, swallowing her cries as he moved inside of her. Faster. Harder. She dug her fingers into the muscles of his back, holding him as close as possible even as she pushed her hips up to meet him.

Tearing his lips from hers, his eyes were burning as he bared his fangs.

Everly knew what he wanted. What he needed. And somehow, she needed it, too. Turning her face away, she exposed her throat.

He struck almost immediately, fangs sinking deep into the side of her neck with a prick of pain. But then he began to drink, and Everly's eyes rolled back in her head, the pleasure so intense it was like strikes of lightening travelling from his bite to her breasts and down to her womb. Another orgasm began to build, stronger than before. His chest vibrated. On a moan? And then one hand slid under her rear, pulling her into each hard thrust as he drank, his hips moving faster and faster as the pleasure rose until her entire body stiffened with tension. She was on fire. Hovering on the edge. Her body screaming for release.

Hawke lifted his head and struck again, deeper this time, and Everly burst into flames as his large body shuddered above her. He pushed as deep as he could go, fangs still embedded in her throat, and Everly lost herself to him.

As his body slowly relaxed, he disengaged from her throat and licked her wound as he continued to slide in and out with lazy strokes. He kissed her jaw, her cheek, her lips, her nose, before he shifted his weight off of her and pulled her against him, tucking her face into his chest and holding her like she was something precious. A gift he couldn't believe he'd received.

Or, maybe she was being overly emotional.

When their breathing had returned somewhat to normal, Everly lifted her head. She wanted to see him. She wanted to tell him how he'd made her feel. Was this normal? If so, then she was making it a new life rule to only date vampires from now on.

His eyes blinked open as the corners of his mouth began to lift in a smile.

It froze on his face as he stared at her, his expression now carefully blank.

The teasing words died in her throat. "Hawke? What is it?"

He slowly lifted her by the shoulders up and off of him, staring at her eyes as if he could find the answers to the universe inside them. He swallowed hard, and his gaze fell to her neck.

He didn't need to say anything. She could feel him leaving her, even though he had yet to move. "What is it?" Icy fingers of dread crawled over her skin as he continued to stare at her. "What's wrong with me?"

No. No! He was fucking seeing things.

But he knew he wasn't.

"Hawke?" Everly reached for him, her touch on his arm both timid and fleeting.

Hawke rolled off the bed and found his pants. He pulled them on with trembling hands, not bothering to fasten them. Balling his fists to stop the damn shaking, his chin fell to his chest.

What the hell did he just do?

He should just walk the fuck out and never look back.

But he couldn't do that. No matter who or what Everly was, she hadn't tricked him on purpose. Her emotions for him were pure. He knew it with every fiber in his being. Because he could feel them, volleying back and forth, now amplified by a bazillion, thanks to her blood in his system. What just happened was no one's fault but his own.

A streetlight came on outside, adding more illumination and breaking him out of his reverie. Something glinted in the corner by the door. Hawke peered closer. It was a thin, gold chain draped into the design of another bohemian-like tapestry covering her wall. He looked around her room. Really looked this time. Gold hung everywhere. On the walls. From the door handles. Draped around the mirror above her dresser. Between that and the bright colors, he felt like he was inside a sultan's jewelry box.

How had he missed it?

Because he'd been too caught up in his physical reaction to her and not thinking, that's fucking why.

"Hawke?" She touched his arm again, and his body reacted despite all the reasons why it shouldn't. Why it can't. Not again.

He stepped out of her reach and covered his face with his hands. "Stupid. Stupid! I'm a fucking idiot!" And he was. The signs had all been there. The lack of fear any normal human would have when confronted with a vampire. The way he couldn't read her thoughts or influence her mind. Her penchant for gold and bright colors...

He'd once known someone else whose room was nearly identical to this one. But it had been a long time since he'd seen her, and he'd almost forgotten—Kohl's mother.

Kohl's *dragon-born* mother.

Kohl's mother who would've been executed for breaking the laws and mating with a vampire, if she hadn't brought with her something the Master had desperately wanted— Kohl. The dragon/vampire crossbreed miraculously born from the union of sin. He was the only reason she'd been allowed to live.

But Everly was deaf. Supernatural creatures did not have disabilities as a rule. It was physically impossible.

Everly pulled his hands away from his face. Her expression was panicked. "Hawke, please talk to me. I don't know what's happening here." She watched his mouth, eagerly waiting for words of reassurance he couldn't bring himself to say.

"Why didn't you tell me?" The question was asked through gritted teeth. *Because she didn't know, you idiot.*

"What?" She frowned, shaking her head slightly. "Please speak clearly. I didn't understand. What?"

Hawke took a deep breath and unclenched his jaw. He asked her again, though he already knew the answer. "Why didn't you tell me?"

"Tell you what?"

"What you are."

The words weren't so much spoken as growled in her direction. But she must've gotten the meaning clear enough, for tears filled her eyes. She took a step back and crossed her arms over her chest. She was wearing his shirt.

A rush of possessiveness filled him. So strong, he could barely comprehend her next words.

"What? Is this some kind of male vampire bullshit because I'm not a virgin or something? I'm not a fucking whore." Her chin rose and she somehow managed to look down her nose at him from her shorter height. "And even if I was, you have no right to judge me for it. Not when guys have been fucking anything with two legs for...*forever* and get nothing but a pat on the back and told what a stud they are."

"What?" It was Hawke's turn to be confused. "No. No. That's not what I'm talking about."

Some of the steel slid from her backbone. "Then what?"

As he studied her face, one tear slid down her cheek, followed quickly by another. She ignored them, didn't acknowledge what she was feeling in any way. Her entire focus was on Hawke, waiting for him to make it better.

She didn't know. He understood this to be true all the way down to his bones. Impossible, you would think. And yet there it was.

It didn't change what he now needed to do. But he could give her as much of an explanation as he could. She deserved that much. He already knew the answer, but still felt the need to ask, "Everly, do you know why Parasupe has your brother?"

A blast of renewed sorrow hit him so hard it took his breath away. Finally, she swiped at her eyes and looked straight at him. "No. I have no idea. I'd only just found him myself when he up and disappeared."

"Was he lost?"

The sarcasm was lost on her. "Sort of." She sighed and walked around him to sit on the bed.

Hawke turned to face her but didn't join her. There were way better things they could be doing on that bed than talking.

Her fingers twisted in her lap, and she said nothing for a

few minutes. But he had all the patience in the world, because he knew once they left this room, this apartment, things would never be the same between them again. So, he waited, drinking in every detail until she looked up at him and began to talk.

"We were separated at birth and both grew up in foster care. I would've never known about him except for these weird memories—*daydreams?*—I'd always had of being around a baby. Later I found out I'm actually older by two years, and those memories weren't just my imagination." A wistful smile softened her features. "I remember the way his face would get all wrinkled up when he'd cry and peeking at him through the bars of his crib when he was sleeping." The smile fell. "But that's about it. Until I started looking into it, I never even knew if they were real or just the creation of a lonely kid who'd always wanted a sibling."

"You grew up in foster homes?"

"Yeah."

Her tone and the careful set of her expression told him a lot about her experiences in the system. "How did you find him?"

"I have some connections, thanks to my job. I got a hold of a copy of the records from when I was first put into foster care." She gave him a smile that took his breath. "I was right. There were two of us." The smile slipped from her face. "We were in the first home together for about a year, and then we got separated and lost track of each other."

Hawke studied her closely, processing every emotion

that now ran through his blood. She was telling him the truth. "Do you know who your birth parents are?"

She shook her head. "No. There was only 'Jane and John Doe' on the records I found. I don't even know if they were alive or dead when the state got a hold of us."

He wanted to ask her more about growing up in foster care. Were her foster parents good to her? Was someone there to help her with her homework? Did they feed her well? Provide for her? Help her deal with her differences? Did they learn to sign? Or did they raise her like any hearing child and that's how she became so good at speaking and reading lips?

But he quashed the urge. That information wasn't important right now.

He went to sit beside her, and she twisted around to face him, bending one leg on the bed. He caught a flash of the heaven between her legs just before she pushed the tails of his shirt down to cover herself and he had to clear his throat. It shouldn't be possible, but he wanted her again. "Everly, I have to tell you something." Because there was no way he could *not* tell her. She deserved that much, at least.

"What? You're married?" Her tone was teasing, but her eyes were worried. "That would really suck, being that you live so long. Or do you have an open marriage? It would make sense." All the fun fell from her face. "Do you live forever? Is that true?"

Hawke huffed out a breath, something between a laugh and a sound of impatience. "Yes. I'll live a really long time, provided no one chops off my head or rips my heart out of my chest." And so will she. "No. I'm not married. Never have been."

"Do vampires even get married?"

"Sometimes. Not normally to each other."

"Why not?"

"Because vampires need human blood"—or shifter blood, as they are more human than vampires—"to survive."

"Oh." She dropped her eyes to her hands where they twisted in her lap.

He dipped his head to catch her attention. "I have to tell you something about your brother, and about you."

She must have noticed the tension gnawing at his shoulders, for the steel was back in her spine and little worry lines appeared between her brows. "What would you know about my brother, or me, for that matter, that I don't already know?"

He ignored her defensive tone. Words jumbled on his tongue until he heaved a sigh and decided the easiest way would just be to show her. So, he got up and went rummaging around in her bathroom until he found a little hand-held mirror. Returning to the bed, he hooked a hand behind her neck and brought her in for a kiss. He meant it to be quick, just enough to re-awaken the passion in her. But his body betrayed him, and by the time he pulled away, they were both fighting for breath.

At least he'd managed to awaken the beast inside of her. Hawke held up the mirror to her face.

At first, she kept her burning eyes on him, on his mouth, ignoring the evidence right in front of her, until he indicated for her to look in the mirror with a nod of his head.

Gray eyes tinged with glowing red fire widened in surprise as she stared at her reflection. Taking the mirror from his hands, she brought it in closer. Then she threw it on the bed and ran over to the mirror on the wall, Hawke's shirt flapping open to either side.

Hawke came up behind her. She was breathtakingly beautiful with her red hair curling in crazy ringlets around her pale face and her bare breasts exposed to his appreciative eye. Eyes the color of a flaming pink sunset flicked up to his face.

Fear tainted her scent and chilled his ardor. *Her* fear.

She stared with horror into the mirror. "Hawke, what is this?"

Unable to stop himself from offering what comfort he could, he pulled her away and took her hands. They trembled violently within his own. He tried to tell her and had to start over twice because her eyes kept drifting back to her reflection. "Do you remember telling me about the winged creature you saw that night?"

She gave him a stiff nod.

"That was my friend, Kohl. The one you met the first night at The Caves."

"Kohl?"

"He's a dragon shifter…among other things."

"A dragon…"

"Shifter. Yes. He has two forms. Like a werewolf."

"I wasn't seeing things."

"No, honey. You weren't."

"What does that have to do with me?"

"It has everything to do with you, because it's what you are. You are a shifter, too, Everly. A dragon, by the looks of it."

She pulled her hands from his, staring at him in horror for a moment before she yanked his shirt tightly around her body to cover herself and walked away. "That's impossible."

When he followed her, she wouldn't look at him, refusing to listen to any more. He ducked down and tried to catch her eyes, and finally took her gently by the chin until she met his gaze. The fire was gone, replaced by icy fear.

"It's not possible." Her tone was pleading. "Please, tell me it's not possible."

"Everly, Parasupe has your brother because he's a dragon shifter. Like Kohl. Like you." He was a fucking idiot not to think about the connection as soon as she'd told him the male he saw in the lab was her brother. Or, maybe he just didn't want to think about it because, like the ass he was, he was too worried about getting his cock wet. "And if they have your brother, they *will* find out about you, especially if you've been sniffing around alerting them to your existence." She pulled her chin from his grasp but didn't walk away this time and continued to read his words. "You can't stay here. It's only a matter of time until they come for you."

"This is my home, Hawke. I have a lease."

"You're gonna break it." The words came from nowhere, but once said, he said it again, because he sure as hell wasn't leaving her here by herself. "You can't stay here."

"I can't do that."

"Yes, you can. And you will."

But she shook her head. "I have an alarm system. I'm perfectly safe."

"Do you seriously think that people who have the facilities to catch people like your brother and keep him caged like an animal would care about a simple alarm system? You should see what I had to go through to even get onto their property without being detected. They'll get past your alarm, Everly. I can get past it. Easily. Any burglar half worth his salt would be able to get past it. You can't stay here alone."

He watched as the truth hit home. "Where will I go?"

"With me." The words were out before he could stop them. What he'd meant to say was 'somewhere safe', or 'to a friend's house'. But, yes. It was the perfect plan. Dragons and vampires did not co-exist, Kohl being the exception. No one would look for her there. She'd be safe at the coven with Kohl leading it. And this way, they could keep an eye on her. Maybe even find out where the rest of her Thunder was located and why she wasn't with them.

He would tell her later about the laws forbidding them to be together. Right now, he needed her cooperation so Parasupe didn't get their claws on her. He would deal with the repercussions from the coven later. "Please, honey. I need you to come with me."

"What about my stuff? My furniture? It's all I have, Hawke. And some of it is special made for my..." She waved a hand in the direction of her ears. "My disability."

"We'll bring everything you need. I'll come back with some of the guys and we'll move it all to the caverns. And don't worry about your lease. This place will be waiting for you when it's over." His chest ached at the thought of bringing her back here, and he had the sneaking suspicion it had nothing to do with her safety and everything to do with the fact that now that he'd had a taste of her, in more ways than one, nothing and no one else would satisfy him.

She looked around and sighed. Then rubbed her forehead. "Okay. Okay. Let me pack a few things."

He gave her a quick kiss, unable to help himself. "Thank you."

Her mouth twisted unhappily. "Where am I going?"

"With me. You're coming to stay with me."

CHAPTER 12

Everly followed Hawke into The Caves. She felt incredibly underdressed in her pajama pants and sweater, but she hadn't thought to put on anything else. She hadn't thought about anything at all the entire way over here. Her mind was completely blank. A self-defense mechanism, perhaps.

Hawke walked around the dance floor, completely ignoring the half-clad women trying desperately to catch his eye and carried her two suitcases into the office. "Stay here," he told her. "Let me go find Kohl and tell him what's going on."

She nodded and sank gratefully into the closest leather chair. Her eyes closed as soon as she laid her head back. She sat there for a few minutes, her body strangely calm. But her mind was buzzing away with everything Hawke had told her back at her apartment.

Could it be true?

But how?

Her eyes popped open. Suddenly restless, Everly got up and walked behind the desk. She opened one of the drawers. It was empty. As were all of the others. Where did they keep their paperwork for the club? The schedules. Anything she could snoop through to get evidence for her story, and to keep her mind off of the terrifying fact that she had some creature lurking inside of her that might burst out any day now.

Any moment.

She trailed her fingers along the desktop as she returned to the chairs. The wood vibrated with the beat of the music playing out in the club. She remembered this one. It was a good song. Contrary to many beliefs, she could "hear" the beat and loved to dance. However, right now dancing was the last thing on her mind. She was too freaked out.

All she could think about were the werewolf movies she'd seen. The way the beast inside of them broke a person's bones and tore through their skin. The way their teeth fell out and regrew and they screamed in pain as their jaw elongated and their legs broke and bent the wrong way.

She froze halfway around the desk and wrapped her arms around herself, pulling her sweater tight, losing the song. The dragon she'd seen was big. Huge, even. And they breathed fire. How the hell was it possible she would turn into one of those things? The blood rushed to her head and she had to sit down. Her heart beat double-time and her skin felt hot and clammy, and she put her head between her legs as panicked tears blurred her vision.

Everly wasn't good with pain. She didn't even have any tattoos. Her ears had been pierced when she was really young, and she still remembered it vividly every time she changed out her earrings. She'd never broken a bone or had so much as a sprained ankle. Once, she'd accidentally slammed her hand in the oven door while checking on the casserole she was cooking, and she'd sat on the floor and cried for thirty minutes.

But she hadn't felt the burn.

Slowly, she sat up and stared down at her right hand. She hadn't opened the door all the way and it had closed on its own as she was pulling her hand out. The heavy thing had slammed shut hard, trapping her hand. She'd been so shocked it had taken her a few seconds to react and open the door again. Her hand had been burned front and back, the skin red and blistered. The oven was old and cranky, and the crush on the fragile bones had hurt like a son of a bitch. But she didn't take much notice of the burns until the next day when Tyson had asked her what happened.

Her heart picked up again and she took deep breaths. That didn't mean anything. She'd probably damaged the nerve endings or something and that was why she hadn't noticed the burns.

Then why were there no scars?

The door opened and Hawke came in, followed closely by Kohl and Devon, as tall and pretty as ever. They filed inside, shutting the door behind them, and came to stand in a circle around the area where she was sitting.

Feeling much like a science project on display, Everly

reached under her hair to discreetly adjust her hearing aids as she stood. It didn't help much, not the standing or the adjusting of her aids. She was still the shortest one there, and she still couldn't hear shit. She didn't know why she even wore the stupid things. They didn't work, other than to separate voices from the other sounds around her. Individual words were impossible to understand. A person speaking to her was just…a sound. There was no tone or pitch to it.

Hawke touched her arm, gaining her attention. She watched his mouth as he spoke, lip reading, and wished she could hear his voice.

"Do you remember Kohl? And you know Devon."

Everly nodded and smiled nervously at Kohl, remembering what Hawke had said about him. She looked him up and down, searching for some sign that it was true, but she didn't see anything except kind brown eyes and muscular arms covered in tattoos beneath his tight blue T-shirt. More tattoos covered his neck, and even the hand he held out for her to shake. She took it and found him smiling warmly at her.

"Hi, Everly."

"Hi."

Then she was engulfed in a cloud of curly black hair as Devon leaned in and gave her a big hug before releasing her. She kept her hands on Everly's shoulders. "Hawke filled us in. Are you doing okay?"

Everly tried to smile at her, but it felt tight and fake. "I'm good."

"No, you're not."

She sniffed and shook her head. "No, I'm not."

Devon hugged her again for long moments before she finally stepped back.

But Everly hung on to Devon like she was the only solid thing in the room and a tornado was about to hit. "This isn't real, right?" she asked her. "This isn't true, what he says about me. It's not possible."

Hawke must've said something, because Devon looked up over Everly's shoulder for a brief moment. She nodded and turned her attention back to Everly. "It's all true. I've seen it," She glanced at the male next to her. "With Kohl. Hell, I've been carried by it."

Everly blinked, thinking she couldn't have understood that correctly.

Devon gave her shoulders a squeeze and dropped her arms back down to her sides, leaving Everly cold and alone. She glanced back at Hawke, wishing he would hold her.

But he just gave her an impersonal smile. "You and Kohl need to spend some time together. He can tell you what to expect."

"Why can't you tell me?"

"Because I'm not a shifter, Everly."

Someone touched her upper arm and she turned to find Kohl trying to get her attention.

"I'm actually still learning about all this myself," he told her. "But I'm more than happy to do what I can to help you." He pulled a cell phone out of his back pocket and checked the time. "The club will be closing soon. Why don't you take her down to the caverns," he told Hawke. "And we'll come down after I make sure everything is locked up."

Hawke must have responded, for Kohl took Devon's hand. But before he left, he told Everly, "We have a lot to talk about, all of us. But feel free to get some sleep if you want. We can talk tomorrow."

"I'm not tired," she said, though she could barely stand without swaying on her feet. "I'll wait for you."

"Okay." Kohl said something to Hawke she didn't quite catch and pulled Devon toward the door.

"It'll be okay," she told Everly as she passed.

When they were gone, she stood staring at the closed door. The air suddenly felt thick and hard to breathe. She could feel Hawke staring at her hard, the weight of it between her shoulder blades nearly bowling her over.

After a few seconds, he appeared in her peripheral vision, walking to the door with her suitcases. His expression was unreadable. With a cock of his head, he indicated for her to come with him.

Everly followed him back out into the club. The dance floor was still packed with too many bodies, and there wasn't an empty table to be found. As they passed close to a group of three on their way around the bar, a young blond man lifted another man's wrist to his mouth. The lights flashed and Everly saw a glimpse of fangs for a brief instant before he bit the guy's arm. His eyes closed as he drank.

Vampires. She'd nearly forgotten she'd be surrounded by them here.

Hawke took her down to the end of another hallway. At

the door, he set down one of her suitcases and laid his palm flat on the reader before opening it.

Everly reached out to take it, but he just shook his head at her and picked it back up, then put his back to the door and held it open for her. As she passed, she tried to catch his eyes, but he kept his head stubbornly down. She found herself on a platform at the top of a metal ramp. It led underground into a dimly lit tunnel of smooth, tan limestone. Her spirit dimmed at the thought of being constantly surrounded by all of this bland stone. But once she reached the bottom, she saw it was much more.

"Oh, my God. It's beautiful," she whispered.

What she previously thought a narrow tunnel actually opened up into a path alongside a small cavern. Stalactites of ancient molten stone hung from the ceiling in long formations. Stalagmites rose from the floor in tall, pointed castles made of dripping particles. The humidity was so thick, a glaze of water shimmered on the floor, the walls, and the ceiling, glittering in the light like tiny golden diamonds.

Everly walked closer and gasped with delight. It wasn't only water that made the walls sparkle. The stone had actual tiny flecks of gold in it. The entire place was like standing in a castle made of gold, albeit a very rustic castle, but a castle nonetheless.

Unable to help herself, Everly spun around to share her delight with Hawke, smiling so big it hurt her face as she gestured to the magic around them.

But he wasn't looking at the gold in the walls or the

impressive columns that seemed to hang mystically in the air. He was looking at her, his body so still he looked to be a part of the stone surrounding them. A predator about to pounce.

Everly caught her breath and her heart began to pound. For a moment, she thought he was about to drop her bags and take her right there on the floor. But then he closed his hungry eyes and visibly inhaled and exhaled. When he opened them again, the embers were still there, but the fire was controlled. "This way," he said. Then he walked as far around her as he could on the narrow path, careful not to brush against her.

Everly followed him, noticing how he didn't look around to appreciate the beauty of the underground cavern. Instead, he kept his eyes directly on the path in front of him and never wavered that she could see.

By the time he veered off through a separate smaller cavern, it felt as if they'd walked a good half-mile through rooms of various sizes and beauty. Up ahead, she caught a brief glimpse of a cavern that was…well, cavernous, and easily as big as a football field, with a throne-like structure in the center of a clearing in the middle of the room, surrounded by a field of stalagmites standing straight at attention. Looking up, she saw a part of the ceiling had been replaced with some type of metal trap door. It was large. Large enough for a dragon to fly through.

She stumbled over the uneven surface, and quickly dropped her eyes when Hawke turned back to check on her so he wouldn't see the shock on her face. Because no matter how many times she'd been told it was true, it still just didn't seem *possible*.

He veered off again down another tunnel, this one so narrow Hawke had to turn sideways a few times to get his broad shoulders through. A few minutes later, and they stopped before a large metal door. Inside was a walled-in room with a bed, a large dresser with a mirror above it, and a comfy looking chair. A book lay open on the nightstand beside it.

Hawke set down her suitcases and finally looked at her. The room smelled familiar, but not like him. And she suddenly realized…this wasn't his room.

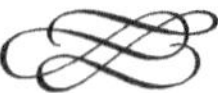

Hawke walked over to stand by the open door, not trusting himself to be closed in another bedroom with Everly.

Despite the fact he couldn't stand the thought of her in another male's room, using another male's shower, sleeping in another male's bed, Kohl's room was the best place to keep her, at least until they knew what they were dealing with. The location of the room, through such a narrow passageway, was ideal in case she shifted when she didn't expect it. And security measures had been taken when Kohl lived there to keep the coven safe from the dragon inside of him. If she did shift, they would have time to get out of the caverns before she managed to bust her way through to the main area.

He knew it was the safest place for her, but he still didn't like leaving her here. It was too far away. Too isolated. If something happened, if someone decided to harass her, he might not hear it. She could be hurt—or dead— by the time he got to her.

Realistically, he knew none of that was likely to happen. The entire coven was loyal to Kohl. More loyal than they had ever been to the Master before him. And even better, they were fucking terrified of him. Well, not of him. But of the beast inside of him who could make an appearance at any moment, especially if they pissed him off. If Kohl told them Everly was not to be touched, they would keep their distance.

But, still, it tore at him.

"Whose room is this?" she asked.

"This is Kohl's room."

She frowned. "I don't want to put anyone out."

"You're not. Kohl and Devon are building a house on his property, and they're staying somewhere else until it gets done."

Glancing around again, she said, "I thought I would be staying with you."

It was hard to ignore the tinge of disappointment in her tone. He pretended not to hear it or understand what it meant. "You'll be all right here," he told her. "I won't let anything happen to you. But I need to keep my people safe."

She looked confused at first, but then her expression cleared as she figured out what he meant by that. "Safe from me." Her voice was barely more than a whisper, and he wasn't sure if she was talking to him or to herself.

He nodded once. "Yes." But she wasn't paying him any mind.

Everly wandered around the room, running her fingers over the plaid comforter on the bed. Touching the dresser. Peeking into the bathroom.

Hawke remained where he was, watching her move around the room in her baggy pajama pants and sweater. She wore the same kind of slip on sneakers all of the human teenagers were wearing these days. Her red hair was pulled into a messy bun on top of her head. Her lips were still red and swollen from his kisses.

But there were new lines of tension around her mouth and in her posture. Her smile, when it came, was timid and unlike her normal Cheshire grin. "Are you going to stay here with me?"

"No. But I won't be far."

She dropped her eyes, but not fast enough. They touched on the bed and back as she made one last ditch effort to make sure she was making herself clear. "I wouldn't mind if you stayed here, too." She laughed a little even as she flushed, blood warming the skin of her chest and neck. "It's not like the bed isn't big enough." The laughter dwindled away. "But I don't want to disrupt your life, either."

Oh, honey. You've already disrupted my life more than you'll ever know. Hawke wasn't ready to have this conversation, not by a long shot, but it was better to just get it over with. "I can't stay here with you, Everly. I can't...we can't be together like we were tonight. Not ever again."

He suddenly felt gutted as the hurt rammed through her and into him. Her expression, however, stayed perfectly composed. It came to him that she was very good at hiding her feelings when she wanted to, probably something she'd perfected growing up the way she had.

"What are you talking about? Why not?"

"Because a mating between a vampire and a dragon is forbidden in our world."

She frowned, watching his mouth closely as he spoke, as though she couldn't be understanding him correctly. "Why?"

"It's an old law, going way back. Our two species can't coexist."

"So, you're saying a vampire and a…" She stumbled a bit over the next words. "…dragon shifter have never hooked up? Ever?"

Well, he'd just backed himself into that corner, hadn't he? "Only once," he told her after a pause.

"And what happened?"

"Kohl happened."

Her mouth fell open comically. "Kohl isn't a dragon? He's a—"

"Hybrid. Half shifter and half dragon, actually."

She stared at him for a minute. "Well, maybe that law needs to be updated." Then she frowned. "And what about Kohl? You said the two species couldn't coexist, yet he's here."

"He is. Because when his mother got pregnant, his father disappeared in shame, and his mother was exiled from her Thunder. It's what dragons call their coven, or pack," he explained at her look of confusion. "She had a contact here, and when the previous Master heard about her—or heard about Kohl, the only one of his kind—he decided to give her and her child shelter. Not out of any feelings of pity for them, but out of the need to be the only coven with a hybrid in its midst."

She thought about that. "If this coven is already different, then maybe…"

"It's forbidden, Everly."

"It's archaic," she corrected. She searched his face, looking for a soft spot, but if she was good at hiding her feelings, Hawke was a master. Even from himself. After a pregnant pause, she muttered, "I see."

Footsteps echoed down the passageway, and Hawke turned his head, breaking the tension between them. Kohl and Devon were coming. Hawke shifted his stance so his back was to Everly and waited for his friends to arrive.

Kohl came around the corner with Devon close on his heels. He looked back and forth between Hawke and Everly. "You okay?" he asked Hawke. "Everything good?"

"Yeah. Everything's fine."

"Then why does Everly look like she just lost her best friend?" Devon asked. "And why is she being locked away down here?"

Hawke exchanged a look with Kohl before he responded. "Because we need to keep her secure until we know what we're dealing with."

Devon looked at him like he'd lost his mind. "What the hell are you talking about?"

Hawke spoke up before Kohl could answer. "Everly is a shifter, Devon. A young shifter. Which means she has no control over that part of her nature. And that makes her dangerous."

"You're dealing with an intelligent woman, not some kind of animal."

Her words stabbed him straight in the chest, sharp as a dagger, but he managed to keep his voice level. Because she was wrong. Everly was an intelligent woman, yes, but she was also a threat to him and his family. "I'm not letting her roam free until one of two things happen." He raised a finger. "One: she goes back to her Thunder. Or, two"—he raised a second finger—"We confirm that she can control her dragon and she's not a threat."

Everly walked up to the group. "I'm right here, you know. And have I mentioned that I am an excellent lip reader?"

Devon turned apologetic eyes her way. "I'm sorry, Ev. Why don't you throw some jeans on and we'll go get something to eat? Are you hungry?" She shooed her toward her suitcases, not really giving her a choice. After Everly found some pants and closed the bathroom door behind her, Devon turned defiant eyes on the two vampires. "I'm taking her for something to eat." She held up her hand, halting whatever Kohl was about to say. "We'll be fine. We'll tag along with Andrew and Frank. They were about to go get something." She was already texting as she said it.

Kohl grabbed her around the back of her neck and pulled her in for a quick, hard kiss. "Please trust me on this one and be careful. I'll catch up with you as soon as I talk to Hawke."

She smiled. "We'll be fine."

He released her, and with a withering look at Hawke, she grabbed Everly and left the two of them alone.

Hawke exchanged a look with Kohl as they listened to the female's footsteps fade away. He knew what was coming, and it was nothing he didn't fucking deserve.

Kohl stared after Devon for a long time, his hands fisted at his sides, before he finally turned to Hawke. "You fucking slept with her, Hawke? What the hell were you thinking?" The words burst from Kohl like water breaking from a dam. "And I thought you said she wasn't a shifter? You swore she wasn't."

Hawke shoved his hands into his hair. "You didn't know, either," he told him. "There was no way I could've known. She showed no signs up until tonight. She doesn't even smell like a shifter!"

Kohl rubbed the back of his neck, a sure sign he was riled up. "Because she hasn't changed yet. No one could tell I am what I am until I changed the first time."

Hawke stared at his friend. "You were younger than she is when you first shifted, and the signs were there long before that." He started pacing the small space. "How can we not sense it? Smell it? And she's fucking deaf! How the hell is this possible?"

"I don't know."

His words barely penetrated as Hawke began to pace in agitation. "Dragons, or any supernatural creature, don't have defects. Ever. How the hell was I supposed to know?"

"Maybe because her brother is a dragon?" Sarcasm

dripped from Kohl's voice. "Maybe because you didn't want to know? Maybe because you wanted to fuck her first?"

Hawke's hand was around Kohl's throat before the last word finished leaving his lips. "Don't you fucking talk about her like that." He was beginning to wish he hadn't filled Kohl in on what he'd found at Parasupe. Or rather, *who*.

Kohl stood his ground, his face turning red from lack of oxygen, and stared Hawke down until he released him with a soft curse.

Kohl took a deep breath, exhaling loudly.

Hawke met his eyes.

"It's forbidden, Hawke."

Hawke was suddenly tired. His head fell forward until his chin rested on his chest. "I know. Why the fuck do you think I brought her here?"

"Why did you bring her here?" Kohl asked with genuine curiosity. "Why not just let her go?"

Hawke gave Kohl a level stare, every cell in his body screaming in revolt as he said, "To do what I have to do to protect our coven and our home."

"Don't you think *not* having a dragon in our midst would do a better job at that?"

"*She* came to *us*."

"To help her break her brother out of Parasupe. Which proves she either has no idea of the bad blood between your species and hers, or she's just playing us. What's to keep them from tracking her here?"

It saddened Hawke that his friend didn't include himself in either of those groups. "They won't find her here, for just that reason. And I will do whatever I have to do to protect the coven, but I firmly believe she didn't know. About her brother, or about herself."

"Good. Because you may need to." He paused. "As soon as we find out what she's really about, she's out. And I'm leaving that mess up to you to take care of." His tone was final. The words of a true leader who had to make hard decisions and stand by them.

Hawke lifted one eyebrow in surprise. "I thought you'd be softer about this. After all, you wouldn't be here if it wasn't for your mom and dad hooking up."

Kohl barked out a derisive laugh and slapped his palms flat against his own chest. "That's exactly it, Hawke. You want to bring another abomination like me into this world?"

"You're not a fucking abomination."

"No? What would you call it, then? I'm a freak of nature. And I would've been dead a long time ago if the Master hadn't taken us in."

"Because he saw you were worth keeping alive."

"Because he wanted to fuck my mom."

Hawke almost forgot about Everly for a second. Almost. "What?"

Kohl laughed bitterly. "Yeah. I was young, but I wasn't stupid. And when he was done with her, he killed her."

This time his attention was all on his friend. "What?"

"Better that than have a grown dragon running loose in his coven." Kohl's shoulders suddenly sagged, and he rubbed the back of his neck. "I can't prove it. But I know

he did. She was healthy. She was fine. And then she…
wasn't."

His friend's pain was plain to see this time. "Why didn't
you ever say anything?"

Another bitter laugh burst from Kohl's throat. "To who?
You? Or one of the other vampires who were so far up the
Master's ass it was a wonder they could piss without his
permission?" He shoved his hands in his pockets and shook
his head. "No. There was no one to tell. And I was too
young to do anything about it. Hell, even if I'd tried, I
would've either been killed or shoved back out into the sun
to be captured by assholes like Parasupe or taken out by
another coven. If I didn't burn alive first."

Hawke felt like an asshole. On an impulse, he grabbed
Kohl in a hug, ignoring his efforts to push him off. "I'm
sorry, man. I really am. I wish I'd known."

Finally, Kohl gave up and hugged him back hard for a
quick second before pushing him away for real this time.
"It's in the past. Nothing you can do about it now. So, don't
worry about it."

Hawke scrubbed his face with his hands. "Fuck." That
was about all he could say to sum up this conversation.

"I'm gonna need to talk to Everly." Kohl paused with one
hand on the lock. "Are you sure she didn't know anything at
all about what's going on with her? Didn't know about her
brother?"

"She only does now because I told her before I brought
her here. But she was completely shocked when I stuck a

mirror in front of her face tonight. If her eyes have done that before, she wasn't aware of it."

"That's how it starts."

Hawke well remembered the horror on Kohl's face the first time it had happened to him. "Yeah."

"And, Hawke?"

"Yeah?"

"Stay the fuck away from Everly." Kohl turned on his heel and stalked off to go find Devon and Everly.

Stay away from the female. Easy, right?

Hawke headed to his room. He needed a cold shower. Maybe it would shock some sense back into him. Because right now, his entire being was screaming in anger and denial for what he would have to do.

CHAPTER 14

Sixteen hours after her dinner with Devon and Kohl, Everly lay wide awake on a strange male's bed, staring up at the glittering ceiling whose beauty no one else seemed to notice or appreciate.

Kohl made her promise to stay in the room, unless he or one of the other vampires escorted her, for her own safety and for the coven's. She supposed it was the smart thing to do, and it gave her a lot of time to think, and shower.

She'd told Kohl everything she could remember about her history, most of which was exactly what she'd told Hawke back at her apartment. No, she didn't know who her parents were. No, she had no idea where she and Matthew came from. No, she didn't know how Parasupe found out about him. Yes, she knew who kidnapped him because she was talking to him on her captioned phone at the time. Everything that was said had been captioned onto her screen, including the visitor's identity when he'd introduced himself to her brother.

Matthew hadn't wanted to go with them, so they'd forced their way in and taken him. On his way out, he'd made sure Everly knew what was going on, right before someone had hung up his phone. The police had been called, but when she'd tried to pull up their conversation to show them, it was gone. Her story had been confirmed with the homeless person who had seen her brother forced from his apartment.

Kohl had promised her they would find out what they could about her brother.

The door opened, and Hawke walked in. His eyes swept the room. Spotting Everly in bed, he came to an abrupt halt.

Everly sat up, swinging her legs off the side of the bed, but said nothing. She didn't have to. Her pounding heart probably gave her away.

His eyes took her in from her bare toes to her messy hair, and then he turned on his heel and left again.

Panic had her jumping to her feet as she tugged her tank top down over her pajama pants. "Hawke!"

But she needn't have worried, for he returned a moment later with a tray bearing covered plates and a large glass of orange juice. The smell of pancakes and bacon filled the room, making Everly's mouth water and her stomach rumble. He set it on the dresser.

"I could really go for some coffee," she told him as her sudden burst of energy dissipated and she sank back down onto the bed. "Seriously. Is there a coffee shop nearby?"

Picking up one of her hearing aids from the table, she put it in her ear.

Hawke turned, spearing her with an impersonal look. "The sun is still up. No one would be able to escort you." His dark eyes were as cold and deep as the rumble of his voice, the expression on his face carefully blank.

Everly didn't understand why he was treating her like this. She hadn't done anything wrong. "I can't help what I am, Hawke. If it's even true," she added as an aside. "And I didn't force you to…to…contaminate yourself by having sex with me. I don't deserve this…*hatred* from you." There was a twinge in her throat on that last part. Her voice may have cracked. But she didn't care. "I can't help who or what I am."

He froze in the act of removing the plate cover, then he turned, and his hand slowly lowered, though he didn't put the cover down. Instead, it dangled awkwardly at his side as he glanced toward the door, the muscles of his jaw working. His words, when they came, must have been hard, because he couldn't face her when he said them.

"Please look at me when you speak," she told him. "I don't know what you're saying."

His head whipped around, and his expression, so drastically changed, nearly gutted her. The blank mask was gone, and in its place was a male in obvious pain. "I don't hate you, Everly."

She jumped to her feet. "Then why are you treating me like this? I may be deaf, but I'm not an idiot, Hawke. And I don't want to hurt anyone. You didn't have to turn me over to Devon and Kohl. You could just talk to me, you know," she finished quietly.

A smile spread across his face, slow and sweet as honey, but it didn't quite reach his eyes. "Talk to you?"

Everly nodded. "*Yes*, Hawke. Talk to me."

His eyes narrowed. Slowly, he twisted around and set the plate cover down next to her breakfast. Or dinner. It didn't really matter down here.

Moving faster than she could track, Hawke was across the room and standing in front of her. Everly gripped his shoulders as he dragged her up against his hard body. One hand tangled in her curls and pulled her head back until she was forced to look up at him.

Hawke snarled at her, fangs flashing. "Talk? Is that what you think I want to do with you? No, Everly." He ran his nose up the side of her throat. Inhaling her scent? And then his eyes were travelling over her face, stopping at her mouth. "Talking is the last thing I want to do right now."

"But…you said we can't do this." A thrill shot through her as he bent his head down to her throat and she felt the scrape of a fang. Her fingers dug into the muscles of his upper arms. "Hawke? You said—"

His eyes, black as night, burned into hers. "I know what I fucking said."

And then he kissed her.

No, 'kissed' wasn't the right word. He ravished her. Consumed her. Until he was the only thing keeping her on her feet. Because there was no way in hell her knees would hold her upright. Not when her bones were melting from the heat.

He kissed his way down her throat, nipping at her collarbone. Goosebumps rose on her skin, and then her tank top was up and off, and her bare breasts were pressed against the soft linen of his shirt. His warm hands ran up her sides to cup the back of her shoulders and he was kissing her again. But only for a few seconds before he was gone.

Everly was left reeling, hands searching the air where Hawke had stood. Opening her eyes, she looked down to find him on his knees before her. Slowly, his hands slid up the backs of her legs, over her ass, and around her hips. His thumbs grazed the crease where her thighs met and Everly swayed with need as moisture pooled there. Her nipples ached, hard as pebbles, and she felt both free and self-conscious with her breasts bare to anyone who might walk in.

Hawke hooked his fingers beneath the waistband of her pants and pulled them down, inch by agonizing inch. She buried her fingers in his hair as he took his time exposing her to his hungry eyes, enjoying the anticipation.

When her pants were around her knees, he tapped on her calf, and she lifted her foot so he could pull off her pant leg. He did the same on the other side.

Everly felt wicked, and slightly embarrassed, standing there completely bare while Hawke was still fully dressed. He tapped the inside of her leg, encouraging her to widen her stance, and when she didn't respond right away, he urged her with kisses that travelled up the inside of her thigh until she slid her foot outward, giving him more room.

He sank his fangs into the soft flesh of her inner thigh, and Everly cried out, a pulse of dark pleasure contracting her lower stomach as he pulled on the vein. He hadn't even touched her *there*, yet, and she was about to come.

Then he was licking and kissing the wounds, his hands digging into her ass, and she felt his tongue, hot and wet, slide back to front along the crease of her sex, pushing through to the tiny little bundle of nerve endings he knew how to manipulate so well. She felt the vibration of his moan as he tasted her, and that was all it took to push her over the edge. Hawke's arms tightened around her thighs and ass, holding her to his mouth as he brought her to orgasm and kept her there until she thought she would scream from the pleasure of it.

When the waves of pleasure dissipated and her heart began to settle back into its normal rhythm, he kissed the curls between her legs as she fought for breath and gently lowered her until she was sitting on the side of the bed behind her, his mouth on her stomach, her breasts, her jaw. He cupped her face between his palms, and when Everly opened her eyes, the sight of Hawke, obviously aroused and needing and flushed from her blood, made her moan.

"How can I stand here and talk to you when that is all I can think about whenever I'm around you?"

"Hawke…" Everly touched his face, and he turned his head, kissing the center of her palm.

"Eat something," he told her. "I'll be back with some more of your stuff in an hour or two." He paused. "You can leave this room if you'd like. But, please," His eyes bore into hers. "Not without me or Kohl being with you."

"I know," she told him sullenly. "To protect me from the other vampires."

"No, love. To protect them from you."

And then he was gone.

CHAPTER 15

Hawke stood outside Kohl's old room, hard as a fucking rock, and telling himself all of the reasons he shouldn't—*couldn't*—go back in there.

Everly's scent was all over him, and not one of them made a fucking bit of sense at the moment.

His phone vibrated in his pocket, and he yanked it out, both grateful and irritated with the distraction. It was Kohl. Devon had finally managed to crack the code and infiltrate the computer system at the lab where Everly's brother was being held. Hawke touched the screen and tapped out that he'd be there as soon as he ran for some of Everly's things, then he shoved his phone back into his pocket. He looked at the door, the only thing keeping him from Everly, and closed his eyes for a moment, fighting down the ache in his gut. Then he set off through the cavern and went above ground.

He managed to avoid getting sucked into any issues

Andrew was having with the stock behind the bar by shoving Devon's friend at him. Frank was more than happy to help out the "cute" bartender by making a run to the nearest liquor store.

Awesome.

Before anyone else could flag him down, Hawke made a beeline to his car. Halfway to Everly's apartment, he realized he'd forgotten to ask her for her key. He'd either have to turn around and go back, get a spare from the landlord, or break in. He weighed the pros and cons of his choices.

Break in it was, then.

Inside her apartment, he quickly deactivated the alarm system. It was entirely too easy. He would have to set her up with a different system before she came back to this apartment.

A low growl rumbled deep in his throat at the thought of her here, unprotected and alone.

If she came back to this apartment.

Hawke gave himself an internal shake. Everly was a grown female, and one of the most dangerous shifters out there. She had no need for a male to protect her. And yet, he knew he would do just that. Always. Whether it be from near or afar, he would watch out for her.

Closing the front door, he turned and glanced around. The first thing to come to him was her scent. Sweet and warm and wild and fucking everywhere. Hawke breathed deep and let her essence soak into him. His body reacted immediately—muscles tensing as his fangs tasted the air, eyes dashing around the room, searching out the woman it belonged to. But then his head caught up, and he sheathed his fangs, knowing the one he wanted wasn't here.

He headed quickly to the back of the apartment. Kohl and Devon were waiting for him to get back, he had no time to fuck around here smelling her underwear like some kind of pervert.

Finding another suitcase in the back of her closet, he threw as many clothes as could fit into it, then went into her bathroom and gathered up her shower supplies and cleaned off her sink, putting it all in a plastic trash bag. He thought about bringing what she had in her fridge, but they had nowhere to keep it cold in the caverns, so he searched her cabinets for stuff that didn't need to be kept cold, then he emptied her refrigerator and took it all out to the trash bin so she wouldn't come home to a stinky apartment. On his way out, he grabbed a patchwork blanket she had thrown over the back of her couch. He stopped at the door, his eyes wandering over to her telephone, but he decided to leave it there. He couldn't take the chance she would accidentally, or purposefully, tell anyone where she was. Besides, if Parasupe was onto her, they could very well have it tapped.

Out at his car, he threw her stuff into the backseat before getting behind the wheel. He sat for a few seconds, searching for signs he was being watched, but not so much as a curtain twitched in the other apartments.

Back at The Caves, he grabbed Everly's stuff from the back seat and went to the office to check in with Kohl and Devon before he took them down to her. The normally empty desk was now covered in two large computer monitors and a keyboard, and Devon sat in front of them with Kohl standing behind her, his arms crossed over his chest and a worried expression on his face as he watched over her shoulder as she typed. They both looked up as Hawke entered, set down the stuff in his arms and closed the door behind him.

"Sorry I took so long. I went to get Everly some things."

"Everything okay at her place?" Kohl asked.

Hawke lifted one shoulder. "Far as I can tell." He made his way around the desk to stand over Devon's other shoulder. "How are things going here?"

Devon's fingers flew over the keyboard. "I've managed to hack into the camera system where her brother is being held and I've been watching all afternoon."

"What about the sound? Can you hear what they're saying?"

She shook her head. "Not yet. I'm working on it now." She glanced over her shoulder at Hawke. "But I don't know that we really need it to see what's going on there."

"What do you mean?"

Kohl answered for her. "We think they're experimenting on him."

"Every couple of hours they do something that affects his muscles or his nerves. He becomes completely immobile while the lab techs go in there and either shoot him up with something or take his vitals. Then they leave, and about an hour later, whatever they did to immobilize him wears off. Once that happens and they're safely out of the cell, they use different methods to rile him up then—hurt him in different ways—until he starts to shift into his dragon form." She hit a key and turned her chair a little to face him. "I think they're trying to find a way to overpower his shifter side, so he *can't* shift."

A red-hot poker went through this stomach. "Have they succeeded?"

"Not yet." Kohl met his eyes.

Hawke held his stare. They both knew what this meant. Earlier, Devon had told him she'd discovered via some intercepted emails that Parasupe was starting to catch shit from the people who funded them for the brutal way they've been "handling" the supernatural community. Namely, taking them out. Normally, they wouldn't have a problem with it, however, humans have been getting caught in the crossfire lately, so they now needed a better way to control them. And they were starting with who they considered the most dangerous—dragon shifters.

Which put the two people he cared about most in this world smack in the middle of their radar.

"What about him?" Hawke pointed at the screen, where Everly's brother was pacing back and forth in all his naked glory, scratching at his face with dirty nails until rivulets of blood dripped to the floor. "Can he be saved?"

Kohl and Devon shared a look, and then Kohl paced away, rubbing the back of his neck. "I don't think so. I don't know what they're doing to him, but I've been watching with Dev for a couple of hours now. I don't think he's…sane anymore. If he ever was."

"According to Everly he was. She said she'd just found

him a few months ago, and they'd been talking." He crossed his arms over his chest and chewed the inside of his cheek as he contemplated the computer monitor with the camera feed on it. "At least, she didn't say anything about him having any sort of mental illness."

"I think we need to ask her," Devon said. "Why don't you bring her up?"

Hawke exchanged glances with Kohl. "Do you think it's safe? I don't want to upset her. There are people here," he added when Kohl raised an eyebrow at him.

Kohl rubbed the back of his neck, looking off in the distance as though he expected to find the answer in the dusty corner. Finally, he sighed. "I don't know."

Devon looked back and forth between the two of them. "Are you kidding me, you guys?" She shoved her chair back and stood up. "What the hell are you going to do? Keep her locked away underground until you decide otherwise? She's not a prisoner here."

Hawke met her eyes and quickly looked away.

She turned to Kohl. "Is she?"

He stared at her for long moments. Hawke waited for what he would say. Kohl was the coven master, after all. If he told him he thought it was safe to let her roam free, then that's what would happen.

Even if Hawke thought it was a really bad fucking idea for reasons he didn't care to explore right now.

Kohl turned to Hawke with obvious reluctance. "Go get Everly and bring her up here."

Hawke gave him a nod and went to pick up her things to

take them down to her. He had one hand on the doorknob when Kohl stopped him.

"And Hawke?"

He glanced back at his friend and leader.

"Keep your fucking hands off her. I'm trusting you. Everly is not yours."

The vampire inside of him hissed a warning, but Hawke managed to keep his voice level as he said, "Threatening me is not *fucking* necessary." Nor would they deter him, as he'd proven just a couple of hours ago.

"Guys." Devon put her hands up, as if to ward off the sudden tension in the room.

Kohl grabbed one and kissed the inside of her wrist without taking his eyes from Hawke. "It's not a threat, man. It's just a reminder."

Hawke's shoulders relaxed as he remembered Kohl's self-hatred from earlier. "You don't have to remind me. I've got things under control."

Kohl stared at him for a moment, the tension slowly leaving his jaw. "Thank you."

With a wink at Devon, Hawke left.

Down in the caverns, Kohl's words echoed over and over in his head.

Everly is not yours.

Everly is not yours.

Fucking funny, because she sure as hell felt like his.

But there was a reason for the old laws. A good reason. Unlike Kohl's mother—who was a very kind female, but weak-willed and easily controlled—once Everly shifted the first time, she would become someone else. Someone who wouldn't like being under the rule of a male who was half her kind. Someone who wouldn't want to be with a male she would see as the weaker of the two species.

When Everly discovered who she truly was, it wouldn't take her long to figure out she was no longer the poor, little, deaf girl.

She could rule them all.

CHAPTER 16

F ed and in her normal attire of jeans and a rainbow T-shirt with her purple sweater tossed over her shoulders and her unruly hair pulled back in a low ponytail, Everly followed Hawke back up to the club.

He'd been more subdued than normal while he'd waited for her to change out of her pajamas, answering her questions with as few words as possible and only looking at her when he absolutely had to. As soon as he could, he'd told her he would wait outside and hauled his ass out of the room.

Everly tried not to be offended. She knew where this all came from. He was beating himself up over what had happened earlier because he refused to see that rules could be changed. She just didn't see the logic in why two supernatural creatures, even if they were different species, couldn't be together. Or anyone, for that matter. It didn't make any sense. If she cared about him and he cared about her, they could make it work.

The real question was, did Hawke care about her?

She stared at the stiff set of his broad shoulders as he opened the door at the top of the ramp and led the way out of the caverns. It was hard to tell. Sometimes, she would swear he did. And other times he made her feel like nothing but a means to an end. The end being finding out information about her brother, who was obviously more of a danger than she ever would have guessed by his shy nature and quiet manner, and why Parasupe had chosen him.

Maybe it was the way vampires worked. If there was a free meal available, they would take it. And if they could get off in the process, then even better. Feelings didn't need to play into it. Not even brand new, experimental feelings.

Everly felt her face heat at her own vulgar thoughts, and she put her hands on her cheeks as they reached the office door. She started when Hawke pulled them away and looked up at him.

"Are you okay?" His dark eyes were filled with concern.

She pulled her hands from his and nodded as she took off her sweater and folded it over her arm. "I'm fine. Just a little warm."

His eyes narrowed as he scanned her from head to toe and back again, but he didn't pursue the topic. Opening the door, he indicated for her to go in first.

Devon grinned from behind the desk, the only one who looked genuinely glad to see her. Everly was surprised to see it covered with actual office stuff, like a computer.

"What's going on?" she asked Kohl, who had pulled one of the comfy chairs around and was sitting beside Devon.

He stood as she and Hawke entered. "Hey, Everly. Did you eat?"

"Yes, thank you."

Hawke steered her toward the remaining chair, but she shook her head. "I'll stand, thanks. I've been sitting or lying down all day." She walked around the desk but stopped before whatever was on the monitors came into view. "What's going on?" she asked again, looking between Devon and Kohl.

Kohl's eyes flicked to Hawke, and Everly followed the direction of his gaze, but only caught the end of whatever he was saying. "...to show her."

"Show me what?" she asked Hawke.

His eyes flicked over to her face and back to Kohl. He didn't answer.

She tried Devon. "Show me what?"

Devon pointed at the monitor on the right. "I've... into..." She stopped and looked up at Hawke, then smiled apologetically at Everly. "Sorry. I forget." She gestured toward her ear and then turned to face Everly full on. "I've managed to hack into the camera of the lab where your brother is being held."

Unexpected tears welled in Everly's eyes and her pulse raced with excitement and nervousness. "You did? You can see him?" She walked the rest of the way around the desk until the monitor came into view, shaking off Hawke's hand on her wrist when he reached for her. She didn't know if he meant to keep her away or was just offering support, but either way scared her even more.

The man on the screen was not her brother. The man on the screen was something out of a horror movie. Naked and dirty and skeletal, he paced the large cell he was in on bare feet that looked too big for the rest of his shrunken body. And yet, he didn't appear weakened at all. Something dark dripped from his fingers and onto the floor, and when he turned so he was facing the camera she saw it was blood from where he'd gouged his own cheeks with his finger-nails. His lips moved, and Everly swiped at her eyes and leaned in to get a better view as Devon rolled back out of her way. For the most part, he was mumbling indistinct words and phrases that made no sense. But every few words she could pick out what he was saying.

Everly straightened. This man was not her brother.

Someone touched her arm. Devon. "I'm sorry I don't have the audio, yet."

"I don't need it," Everly told her. "He's...he's just babbling. Mostly."

Hawke came into her line of view. "Can you understand anything else?"

Tears warmed her eyes again. "Mostly, he wants to kill everyone there. He wants to kill himself." She didn't want to tell him what else Matthew had said, but he came around the desk and took her by the shoulders, turning her to face him. Ducking his head, he caught her eyes with his. "What else is he saying, Everly?"

She looked away, but he took her by the chin and forced

her to look at him. Tears spilled over and rolled down her cheeks as she felt the pressure of his mind poking at her brain. "He blames me for what's happening to him." She waved her hand at his face. "Stop that."

He cocked his head to the side as he studied her, but then the pressure disappeared. "Why is he blaming you?"

"Because if I had never found him and made him come here, they wouldn't have found him, either."

Kohl got her attention. "Everly, did he—Matthew, is it?"

She nodded.

"Did Matthew know? Did he know what he is before Parasupe got a hold of him?"

Her immediate response was to shake her head. But then she stopped, because she honestly didn't know. "I have no idea. He never said anything to me about it if he did."

Hawke dropped his hands from her and took a step back. He and Kohl stared at each other over her head, communicating without saying a word.

"What?" she asked as she looked between them. "What?" she asked again, louder now.

"Are you hungry?" Hawke asked her. "We can go get some food."

Everly threw both hands in the air, palms out to each of the males. "I just ate and you know it. If one of you doesn't tell me right *now* what the hell is going on..."

She looked at Kohl, who looked at Hawke. Desperate for some kind of an answer, she turned to Devon.

"You guys need to tell her," she said, looking directly at Everly.

"Tell me *what?*" She turned to Hawke. He was the one she wanted answers from. He would be honest with her. Somehow, she knew that.

His chest rose and fell with each steady breath. "Everly, we're going after Parasupe. Particularly this lab. We've been planning it for a while now, and with Devon's help, we now have a lot of information we didn't have before. No one should ever have to go through what this male is going through right now."

"This male," she repeated. "You mean my brother."

His eyes travelled from her eyes to her lips and back. She had no idea what he was thinking, so she waited.

"Your *brother* is out of control, Everly. He's a danger to himself and anyone around him now. It isn't his fault. Who the fuck knows what they've been shooting him up with all these weeks, but I can almost guarantee they have a tracking device implanted in him somewhere. Even if he happens to get out, they'll find him. And if he's with you, they'll find you. He needs to be...taken out of the equation."

It took her a good five seconds to process what he was saying. She immediately shook her head. "No. That's not happening. He's my brother. My only family."

"It has to happen. I'm sorry."

Everly stared at him. Stared at this male who made her feel so many different things she'd never experienced before. Somehow, she never thought hatred would be one of them. "I'm not letting you hurt my brother. He's all I have."

Hawke started to say something but stopped. His eyes travelled over her face before landing on her own and staying there. There was something about the way he was looking at her...

Kohl was stepping between them. "Everly, you need to calm down."

She turned her anger on him. "Don't tell me how to feel, Kohl. You three are all standing here telling me you're going to kill my only family and you expect me to be *calm?*"

Devon took her hand, getting her attention. "What he's trying to say is you're showing signs of shifting, and we can't have you spreading your dragon wings in here. You'll take out half the club."

Shifting? Everly looked between Kohl and Devon, purposefully ignoring Hawke. Now that she was paying attention, the back of her neck was on fire. She reached up to rub it away. Was that a sign?

Her heart began to race. It would hurt like hell, there was no way it wouldn't. Her chest burned like she had a severe case of heartburn, and she suddenly couldn't catch her breath. She reached out for something to stabilize her as the room faded in and out of her vision. Her hand was grabbed and held tight, and then she was being lowered to a chair. Warm palms cupped each side of her head, and when she opened her eyes, all she saw was Hawke. She tried to concentrate on his face.

"Get out. I got this."

She frowned, and then realized he was talking to Kohl and Devon. Kohl must've argued with him, for he bared his fangs without taking his eyes from her and told them again to leave, adding, "In case you've forgotten, this isn't my first time dealing with a young shifter."

So, now she was something to be *dealt* with?

Something rumbled in her throat. A sound she felt but couldn't hear. But she hadn't consciously made it. It happened all on its own. Her insides stirred unnaturally, like something was alive in there. Everly clasped her stomach and fought Hawke's grip.

"Everly. Everly, you have to control it." Hawke's hands tightened a bit on her face, forcing her to still. "You can do it."

She was having a hard time focusing on his words.

"If you don't control it, you're going to shift right here in the office." He paused. "It's very possible you'll kill everyone here." He paused again. "Well"—one side of his mouth twisted into a humorless grin—"maybe not Kohl."

"You should leave." Her throat felt too thick. She had no idea if the warning she'd tried to give him was understandable. "I don't know what's happening."

"I'm not going anywhere, honey. If you want to take somebody out, it's gonna be me."

The rapid pounding of her heartbeat was loud in Hawke's ears. Iridescent colors rippled up and down the exposed skin of her arms and neck in waves. The bones in her face shifted slightly under her skin. And her eyes glowed with pink fire. Everly moaned, on the verge of her first shift, and he was terrified for her.

She didn't know to go with the change. She would fight it, like Kohl had, and it would cause her more pain than was necessary. Hawke forced himself to steel his nerves. It wouldn't do any good to freak out along with her.

The door clicked softly as Kohl removed Devon from the room. Hawke knew he was probably sending her below ground until he knew it was safe. He returned a few seconds later.

Still holding Everly's face between his hands, Hawke shook his head just enough for him to see.

"I'll be right outside," Kohl told him. "Do I need to clear out the club?"

"Not yet," Hawke told him. "Everly, I need you to focus. Focus on me and breathe. Just breathe."

Shadows shifted behind her eyes, and someone—or some *thing*—else looked out at him.

This wasn't good. She would have to shift eventually, but it would be better to do it in a controlled environment, like out in the middle of fucking nowhere. Not inside the club.

He heard the door close again and decided to try a different tactic. "You know, when Kohl shifts, the creature he becomes doesn't recognize me. Or anyone he's close to, really." He thought about that for a moment. "Except Devon," he corrected. "He recognizes Devon. He even saved her once while in his shifter form when some vampires from our coven followed them out to his property one night. He burned three of them alive—don't look at me like that, they were assholes—then he swooped in and picked Devon up as she ran away from a fourth and flew with her to his favorite field. The dragon side of him is fond of soaking up the warmth of the morning sun." He paused. Her eyes, burning and watery, stayed glued to his face. His distraction appeared to be working.

She frowned at him, her tongue still sounding a bit thick for her mouth as she said, "How can he sunbathe if he's half vampire?"

"He can't. That's the thing. He ends up passing out, and when he wakes up back in his normal form, he has to run like hell to the closest shelter before he bursts into flames."

Her eyes, still teary but tinged with only the slightest wisps of fire now, widened in fear for a male she barely knew. Hawke rubbed her temples with his thumbs. When he felt her begin to relax, he released her face. Immediately, her teeth began to chatter, and gooseflesh covered her arms as the heat of her almost-change subsided.

She rubbed her arms. "That would be terrifying. Can't he tell the thing inside him not to take him there?"

Hawke smiled as her cheeks reclaimed their normal color. "It appears his dragon has a mind of its own."

She drew back, tilting her head to the side as she pulled her sweater back on. "Will I recognize you?"

He gave her a little shrug. "Guess we'll eventually find out." He looked her over. "But not today, it seems."

Her jaw tightened, halting the chattering. Before Hawke could think of what to say that would help put things in perspective, she asked, "Do vampires feel anything? Other than thirst?"

The question, completely off topic, threw him for a bit of a loop. He studied a soft, red curl lying along the curve of her cheekbone. Right at this moment, Hawke was feeling way more than he should. He was feeling so many things he was worried it was going to affect his judgment when the time came to do what he needed to do with her brother—and at some point in time, possibly her.

He should tell her what she expected to hear. Tell her what he should to end this thing between them right now. The lie was right there, on the tip of his tongue…

But he couldn't bring himself to tell it.

"I feel things," he told her when she finally got up the courage to look at him for an answer.

Her eyes, clear as the morning sky just before dawn, searched his face. "Do you feel anything…for me? Other than the urge to drink my blood." Her tone was teasing but her emotions didn't match. No. Her emotions were dead serious.

Though he knew the entire time where she was headed with this, the question hit him right in the gut. Maybe it was the way she held herself so carefully, like she would shatter into tiny pieces if he touched her. Maybe it was the set of her jaw and the way she so carefully and distinctly pronounced each word. Or maybe it was the way a fire of a different kind all together burned through the mist in her gray eyes.

Maybe it was because he'd been through enough shit in his long life to know he shouldn't—couldn't—have *any* kind of feelings for this female.

And, yet, he did.

Only they weren't simple "feelings." They were fucking cyclones of emotion that raged through him every time the faintest whisper of her scent reached him. Every time he heard her laugh. Every time she lit up a room simply with her aura. It seemed impossible after so short a time, and yet, there it was.

Hawke straightened, setting himself away from her. He needed to regain control of this conversation. "My feelings for you, or lack thereof, aren't important right now."

"They're important to me."

"It won't change anything."

"Because you don't want it to."

"Because it's not possible."

She was silent then, but the way she looked at him spoke volumes.

Hawke sighed and rubbed his forehead. "Everly, sometimes hard choices have to be made."

She stood and pulled his hand away from his face. Her mouth twisted into something resembling a snarl, and he blinked in surprise. "Don't tell me about hard choices, Hawke. I know all about them. Every choice I've ever made in my life has been hard except for—" She snapped her mouth closed abruptly.

"Except for what?" Was it wrong that his heart pounded in anticipation? Should he despise himself for being so weak that he wanted to hear the words? "Except for *what*, Everly?"

"Except for the choice to be with you," she whispered. "That choice was easy. It was right. And nothing you say will ever convince me otherwise."

He inhaled sharply in an attempt to clear his head, and her sweet scent filled him. Hawke froze and ground his teeth together, keeping his fangs concealed. But it was no use. This female with her questions and her imperfect smile and her laughing eyes had burrowed her way under his skin. It was more than the bloodlust, more than the sex. It was the way she embraced her life with a joy he hadn't felt in a long time. It was the way she flayed him open with her frank honesty. The way she cared for a brother she barely knew. The way she gave herself openly, trusting him not to hurt her.

Hawke couldn't lie to her. Not when she stared at him with her heart in her eyes. He took her hands, pressing his forehead to hers briefly. "This thing between us, whatever it is, it has to stop." He raised a hand when she was about to argue. "It has to stop. You'll hate me when this is all over."

"No, I won't."

He pulled back to see her expression better. Something fluttered in his gut. A warning, perhaps. "You won't?"

"No." Rising up on her tiptoes, she pressed a kiss to his lips. "Because you're not killing my brother."

Pain lanced through his skull. His vision cleared just in time to see Everly throw the keyboard back on the desk and turn to run. If nothing else convinced him she was a shifter, the strength in that hit just fucking did.

He caught her before she made it to the door, spinning her around and wrapping his arms around her. She struggled, but he wouldn't release her. Kohl was standing right outside. Hawke was actually surprised he hadn't come in yet. Even over the music, he should've heard the commotion.

When she finally realized her plan was thwarted and she wasn't getting away, she took a deep breath, the movement pressing her breasts against his chest, and lifted her chin. "Let me go."

Hawke knew she wasn't talking about being in his arms. Not entirely. "I can't do that, honey."

"Why not? I'll go get my brother myself."

"And then what are you going to do?" She wriggled in his hold, and he released her, hanging on to her hand when she would've walked away. "Before you think of smashing that monitor over my head next, you should know that Kohl is right outside that door. Even if you manage to knock me out—which isn't likely—you won't get very far."

Everly pulled her hand away and walked around the desk to stare down at the camera feed. A tear escaped to run down her cheek and she quickly dashed it away.

Hawke pushed his hair back out of his face. He had no idea what to say or do to make her feel better. And maybe there was nothing he *could* say. The situation was what it was. And sometimes hard choices had to be made. All he knew was there was no way in hell he was allowing her to go after her brother alone so she could go off and get herself hurt…or killed. He'd known who Everly was when Hawke had mentioned her, but with him getting shot up with whatever the fuck it was Parasupe was injecting him with, that could all be different now. When Hawke saw him just forty-eight hours ago, he could still talk coherently. Not so much today. The gods only knew what condition his mind was in.

As though she knew exactly what he was thinking, Everly said quietly, "He's my brother, Hawke. Wouldn't you do everything you could to help Kohl?"

"That's different."

She laughed without humor. "It's not different, and you damn well know it. What if it was Kohl stuck in that cell? Don't stand there and tell me you wouldn't try to get him out. That you wouldn't try to help him no matter what they'd done to him." She waited expectantly.

Hawke opened his mouth to deny it, but in the end, he knew she was right. "What do you want me to do, Everly? I can't just walk in there and set him loose, even if I wanted to."

"What would you do if it were Kohl?"

He shook his head. "I have no fucking idea."

"But you would get him out."

He scrubbed at his face. She had him there. He couldn't lie to her about it. Letting his arms fall back to his sides, he said, "I would try."

But she wasn't done. "And what if it were Kohl who was out of his mind and couldn't control his anger?"

Hawke didn't even have to think about it. "I would put him down before he could hurt anyone. And I would mourn him with the respect he deserves."

She stared at him for long seconds, and then she sank into the office chair and put her head in her hands.

Hawke went to her and gently pulled them away. When she raised her head, he saw tears were running silently down her cheeks. He brushed them away. "I'm sorry, honey. I wish I could tell you something different. But I'm not going to lie to you about what could very well turn out to be a very fucked up situation."

She gave him a sad smile. "I do appreciate that. Even if I don't want to hear it."

He pushed a red curl back from her face. "We're going to take out that fucking laboratory, and if we can save your brother, we will. But I will not allow him to hurt anyone. I will not allow him to hurt *you*. On that, you have my word."

CHAPTER 18

Later that night, after the club closed down and Kohl and Devon went back to their temporary home, Everly sat at the empty bar while Hawke locked up and waited for Andrew to count the till, and then walked with him back down into the caverns. They passed a few other vampires who had been working that night, probably on their way to go feed. But they didn't give Everly more than a cursory glance.

Still, staying in the middle of a coven of vampires wasn't the most stress-free environment. She wished Hawke would stay with her, or let her stay with him, but she knew it wouldn't happen. He didn't even have to say anything, his body language said it all.

When they got to her room, Hawke hesitated in the doorway as Everly went in and switched on the bedside lamp. Her hand shook, and she tucked it into the pocket of her sweater though she didn't know why she bothered. He never missed anything.

She stood there awkwardly, purposefully avoiding his gaze so he couldn't say goodbye and leave her. But after a minute or so, he crossed the threshold and came to stand before her, and then she had to look at him so as not to be rude.

"Is there anything you need before I go?"

Everly started to shake her head, but then she stopped. "Would you stay for bit? Keep me company?"

He became very still, in the way she was discovering only vampires could. "I don't know if that's a good idea."

"Please? We can just talk." She paused. "It's just that I'm not really tired and I could really use the distraction."

"Talk." He made a face when he said the word like it left a bad taste on his tongue.

"Yes. Talk. Please?"

He turned his head away as he said something, and she didn't quite catch it all. But it looked something like, "I'm not even supposed to be here with you."

"Hawke?"

His chest rose and fell on a breath. Nodding his head slightly, he walked around her and sat down in the chair beside the bed. Idly, he picked up the book laying there—a historical about WWII from the looks of it. Putting it back, he gave her an impersonal smile. "What would you like to talk about?"

Everly kicked off her shoes and climbed up onto the bed. She hadn't really expected him to stay, and now that she had him here, she had no idea what to say. "Why don't you tell me about your life. It's gotta be a lot more interesting than mine."

"My life." He scraped his fingertips through his beard. "What would you like to know?"

Everly shrugged. "Everything. When were you born? Where are you from? What's it like being a vampire?"

He studied her for a few seconds. Then he leaned forward and rested his elbows on his knees. Tonight, he wore a tangerine shirt and black slacks, and with his dark hair and beard, the combination was absolutely yummy. "It's…" He paused for a long time. "Monotonous."

She couldn't help it. She laughed. "Monotonous?" It wasn't the answer she would have expected from someone who had the time and the money to do anything he pleased.

A smile teased the corners of his mouth. It didn't reach his eyes. "Yes." His chest rose and fell on a deep sigh. "Vampires live the same day over and over and over again. I look the same. I feel the same. My diet never changes." At this, the smile broadened before it slowly slid away. "People are born, and people die. Cities rise and fall. The technology improves. The seasons change. But in the end, it's all the same. You wake, you feed, you find ways to amuse yourself, you avoid those who would hunt you, you hide from the sun. And then tomorrow you start all over again."

He glanced at her, eyes shifting away again as though he hadn't meant to say so much, waving away his words as if they meant nothing. But she could see the sadness in his words. "To answer your first question, I've lived a long time. Long enough to sound like a grouchy old man."

She gave him a moment to come back from wherever his head was. "Are you from America?"

"No. I was born a vampire in Europe."

"What about before that? You were human before you were a vampire, right?"

"No. I was born a vampire. Just as you were born a dragon."

Everly was stunned. "So, you weren't turned? You can't turn someone else?"

Hawke shook his head. "No. But that's probably a good thing. Many stupid decisions probably would've been made before I was old enough to realize the true meaning of having children."

Fascinated with this up close and personal supernatural history lesson, she asked, "What brought you here to the states?"

"My brother." He stared down at the floor. "He was my half-brother, actually. We didn't advertise our relationship." Something resembling a smile twisted his mouth. "His choice. Not mine. Although I was glad for it in his later years."

"Why is that?"

"Because he was batshit crazy." Leaning back in his chair, he shrugged it off. "We parted ways for a long time. Then word came to me that he was Master of his own misfit coven in a place you would never expect vampires to live. It made a stupid kind of sense, though. Living in the middle of a place early settlers called hell itself, and so I joined him."

Everly looked around the living quarters she was in. "This place? Your brother—sorry, half brother—was the Master of this coven?"

Hawke nodded. "Yeah."

"I thought Kohl killed the last Master?"

"He did."

"And you did nothing about it?"

He looked at her like the thought had never occurred to him. "And what would you expect me to do? Avenge him? He brought it on himself. Kohl challenged him and won. It was a fair fight. The coven has accepted him as their new Master."

She thought about that for a moment. "Isn't there some kind of rule of lineage, though? Like royal families? Whoever has the same blood as the previous Master gets the throne?" It made sense, though she had no idea if this was true or not.

His only response was to shrug, which told Everly she'd hit it right on the mark.

"Hawke, if you should be Master of this coven, why not take your rightful place?" And, if *he* was the one who made the rules, then they could be changed. Like the rule about dragons and vampires not being able to "co-exist".

But he either didn't see the possibilities, or he didn't care enough to fight for a chance with her, for he only said, "I'm not cut out to lead anyone."

Everly asked him to repeat himself, thinking she couldn't

possibly have understood that correctly. She may have only known Hawke for a short time, but she'd seen him in action. He was confident and capable and kind, but strong when he needed to be. It seemed like a strange thing to say about a vampire, but all night she'd watched from her bar stool as others had come to him about issues, and he'd handled them all with a calm, fair logic she envied. And modesty wasn't one of his strong points, so it wasn't some misplaced sense of humility he was coming from. "What makes you think that?"

"Because I had the honor of that title once. It...didn't work out well."

She just couldn't see it. To her inexperienced eyes, he was the epitome of a leader. "I can't believe that. Everyone makes mistakes, Hawke—"

"Let it go, Everly."

But she shook her head. "No, I won't. As I said, everyone makes mistakes, but that's no reason to—"

Though his face had the same expression as before, his eyes burned with emotion. "A mistake that leads your entire coven to their death? A mistake that spares you only because you're too cowardly to lead them? A mistake?" He threw his head back, mouth open. With laughter? With rage? "The only mistake was ever thinking I could be responsible for keeping them safe."

"I find that hard to believe," she said, adding on before he could say anything else, "But I wasn't there. I don't know what happened or how true that may or may not be."

"No, you weren't." He scooted to the edge of the chair,

dark eyes intense, mouth twisted in disgust. "My entire coven was trapped and slaughtered within the village where we hunted. The humans were waiting for us with torches. They'd poisoned their blood with a venom so toxic it temporarily weakened us, and then they burned my family alive while they writhed in pain." Hawke paused, chest heaving as though he'd just run for miles. Sweat broke out on his forehead, and his hands clenched into tight fists. "It may have only been one decision, but it was a decision that wiped out my entire coven." He looked as though he was about to say more, then with a start, as though just remembering she was there, he sat back. "But no, you weren't there."

She wanted to reach out to him, comfort him somehow, but instinct told her her efforts wouldn't be well received. So, she decided to try a different tactic. "There's one thing I don't understand, though."

Crossing his arms over his chest, he cocked his head to the side and waited. His eyes shifted to the door once with an air of impatience.

Scooting to the edge of the bed, she mimicked his pose from before. "If Kohl is the coven Master, and he's half vampire and half dragon, why hasn't he tried to change the laws pertaining to the two species?"

"Because Kohl believes his existence is a curse, and he would never wish it upon anyone else."

Everly scowled. "That's ridiculous."

Again with the shrug. "He has a point. Even if we changed the rules for this coven, others wouldn't understand. We would be under constant scrutiny. Covens who are our allies now would want nothing to do with us. Dragon Thunders, either. When threats like Parasupe happened, no one would be watching our backs."

"But—"

He slashed his hand through the air. "Stop."

She pulled back, surprised by his outburst and honestly, a little hurt.

He must have noticed, for he visibly exhaled, allowing the tension to leave his body. "I'm sorry," he told her. "But there's no sense in going round and round about this. I know what you're doing, and I wish things were different. I do. Right now, I would love nothing more than to pursue this thing that's started between us. To say fuck the laws and pull you onto my lap and show you all of the ways I would love to worship you. Talk with you about everything and nothing. Watch you grow into your wings. Tell everyone to fuck off and run away with you."

Warmth filled her at the images he created. "But?"

"But we can't do that, honey. Our kind needs others like ourselves around us, for support and protection. Our people—my coven and your Thunder—are why we've survived this long in this world overrun by humans. We wouldn't make it long on our own."

"I don't know about that," she told him. "I've survived just fine on my own up until now."

"I can tell by your desperate need to find your brother."

He smirked, and she scowled. "That's not fair."

"Maybe not. But it proves my point. Your instincts led

you to search for him. They know you need to be around others of your kind."

She leaned toward him again. "I need to be around you." There. The truth was out. Her cheeks burned, but she wouldn't take them back or look away and pretend she'd never said it. "I don't know about instincts, but something keeps telling me I need *you*, Hawke."

Gently, he brushed her hair back from her face. "It's getting late. You should get some sleep."

She didn't want to sleep. She wanted him to finish what he'd started earlier. But she knew he wouldn't. Just like she knew pressing him any more on this subject would only deepen the divide forming between them. "Would you stay just a little longer?"

"Only if you promise to try to sleep."

With a grin and a "be right back," she jumped up from the bed and went into the bathroom to put her pajamas on and brush her teeth. When she came out, he'd turned down the lamp and made himself comfortable in the chair.

After Everly climbed into bed, he asked her to tell him more about her childhood. She did, glossing over the unpleasant parts of being in foster care and focusing on the good years. She told him everything she could remember, none of which was any use in discovering who her real parents were. And eventually, she fell asleep with tears in her eyes and the back of her knuckles against the warmth of his leg.

When she woke up, he was gone, and a ripe peach lay on the nightstand beside the book.

Everly picked it up, inhaling the unique scent before she took a bite of the sweet fruit. Then she got up and went to the bathroom to shower and dress. She needed to go up to the office and check on her brother. Hopefully everyone else was already awake and decided on a plan to get him out of there. Or at least Devon. If she was there, perhaps she could talk to her and convince her to help her talk the guys into giving him a chance before they went all jury and executioner on him. Her heart ached as she thought of the only other alternative.

Because if they wouldn't agree to it, then she knew what she would have to do.

CHAPTER 19

Hawke paced his room. Everly had fallen asleep hours ago. He'd sat with her for a long time before he'd left, listening to her delicate snores, watching every little twitch and flutter of her eyelids.

He wondered if she could hear the music she so loved to dance to in her dreams.

It came to him that he'd never asked her how she'd lost her hearing, if she was born that way or if it was from some type of injury. Then again, the how and why of it didn't really matter now. Alone, in his room, he could be honest with himself and admit that even if he'd figured out her heritage earlier, it wouldn't have mattered to him either way. He still wouldn't have passed up the chance to be with her. He craved her even now.

They'd talked for a long time tonight, and Hawke was completely convinced she had no idea at all who she was or where she came from. Only who she became after she was adopted into the system. Her brother, on the other hand, was another story. She'd talked about him a lot, told Hawke how she'd found him, what their reunion had been like, how happy she'd been to find this link to family. Her eyes had filled with tears as she'd remembered, but she'd wiped them away before they could spill over.

In the end, it didn't change anything. No matter what he'd been through or was going through now, they had to think of the safety of the coven, and he was a hell of a lot more dangerous to their existence than Everly.

Giving up on the idea of sleep, he made his way above ground. As it was still daylight out, he opened the door an inch at a time as he always did when he was the first one to come up. Caution was the reason he'd lived as long as he had. The club was dark and empty, everything intact. Closing the door behind him, Hawke went to the office and collapsed into the desk chair.

Everly's brother paced his cell with erratic jerks of his body. Occasionally, he would rush from one end to the other with a sudden burst of speed. When he turned, Hawke saw white bone partially jutting through the skin of his back. As he came back toward the camera, he looked up for only a fleeting moment before he twisted around and rushed to the other end, but it was enough for Hawke to see the glow of his eyes and the misshapen shape of his face.

He took deep, calming breaths as he hit some keys and scanned the room with the camera. The lab was empty, all the scientists gone for the night. The fucking bastards.

They'd left him like that, partially shifted, his features twisted in agony.

Hawke sat back in his chair and scratched at the scruff on his face with both hands. He actually felt a twinge of pity for her brother. Matthew? Is that what she said his name was? If he wasn't fucking crazy before, he sure as hell would be now.

"Damn it." Despite what he'd told Everly earlier, he'd been hanging on to a slim thread of hope that he would be able to deliver her brother back to her intact and unharmed. His reasons were nothing short of selfish. He wanted to be her hero. What happened to the male after that would depend on if he had been as naïve as Everly about his other half. If so, perhaps Kohl would decide to just let him go, once he knew neither of them meant any harm to the coven.

Problem was, Hawke was no longer so sure he could say the same about his sister.

As if she knew he was thinking about her, Everly opened the office door. Her eyes were red and her skin was blotchy, like she'd been crying. Spotting Hawke sitting behind the desk, she closed it behind her and joined him.

He didn't try to hide the camera feed from her. It was better for her to see it. Hiding things like this from people didn't achieve anything. She would find out sooner or later, and then she would turn her anger on him for not telling her what was happening with her brother.

"What's wrong with him?" Her voice shook, and she cleared her throat. "What is that on his back?" She turned to Hawke with horror-filled eyes.

Though it was quite obvious, he told her anyway. "Those are his wings," he told her. "Or a part of them."

"Why are they like that?"

Hawke watched the creature in the cell for a few moments. "It looks like they've succeeded, at least partially, in finding a way to keep him from shifting. And I say partially, because, as you can see, he started to turn. But they stopped it somehow. My guess is it won't be long until he won't be able to shift at all."

"And then what will they do to him?"

He turned in his chair to face her. "I don't know for sure."

But she wasn't fooled. "They're going to kill him, aren't they?"

"If I had to guess, I would hope so. Because his other option is staying right where he is and continuing to be their lab rat." He touched the back of her hand with his fingertips, and then let his arm fall back to his lap. "I'm sorry, Ev. I really am. I wish there was something else we could do. But the only thing I can offer is to take him out quick so he doesn't suffer anymore." Hawke was surprised to find he truly meant it, if for no other reason than to see her truly smile again.

Little lines appeared between her brows as she studied him. "That's the first time you've called me that." Then she turned and stared at the monitor as she said, "What about me?"

With her attention diverted, Hawke allowed himself the time to drink her in, from the top of her curly head to the sweet curve of her ass and all the way down to her sneakers. He smiled when he saw they were purple this time, but still sparkly. When he looked up again, he was met with the cloudy sorrow of her stare. "What's going to happen to me when this is all over?"

"I don't know," he told her honestly.

"Will you 'take care of' me, too? Put me out of my misery?"

No. No, he couldn't do that. He wouldn't do that. Turning his chair toward her, he slid his hands up the outside of her thighs and gripped her hips. He opened his mouth to reassure her, but the words wouldn't come. So, he ended up pulling her toward him until he could rest his head in the soft curve of her stomach. Inhaling deeply, he breathed in her scent, sweet and warm, and exhaled through his mouth. It soothed him, if only for the moment. But it also excited him. He touched the tips of his fangs with his tongue, knowing it would only jack him up more, but he did it anyway. It was a poor substitute for the salty sweetness of her skin, the silky slide into her body, but it was all he would allow himself.

After a few seconds, her hands tangled in his hair. He thought she was going to push him away. Instead, she held him to her and spoke to the top of his head. "I know we haven't known each other very long, but I have to be honest with you."

He squeezed his eyes closed as his fingers dug into her supple flesh. "Don't say it," he whispered, knowing full well she wouldn't hear him. "Don't say it."

But she did say it. And every word made his breath quicken and his petrified vampire heart pound with new life, longing for something that wasn't now, and would never be, possible.

"I don't want to leave you, Hawke. I've never felt so…" She faltered, and then the words poured out, tumbling over themselves. "*At home* as I do in your arms. I've never felt so much a part of someone as I do when you're inside of me, when you take my blood inside of you. I've never been with a man I feel so safe with. I trust you completely, with my safety, with my body, with…everything. I'm not naïve, Hawke. I'm not a young girl who just loves to be in love. But I think…no, I *know*, there's something between us that doesn't happen everyday." Her stomach rose and fell as she took a deep breath. "And you're a fucking idiot if you don't think it's worth fighting for. I'm not giving up that easy."

He stayed where he was, knowing the moment would have to end and he would have to crush her dream—again— of anything happening between them.

"I'm not giving up on you. And I'm not giving up on my brother."

Fuck.

Hawke removed his hands from her hips and leaned back in the chair so she could see what he was saying. He spoke slowly, pronouncing every word distinctly, so there would be no misunderstanding. "That's not happening, Everly. Not with me. And not with your brother. You have to let him go."

She shook her head, red curls swinging. "No. I won't."

"Everly."

"No!" Covering her face with her hands, she took a few breaths. "I've been alone my entire life, Hawke," she said through her fingers. Then she dropped her arms to her sides. "Don't you get it? Do you know what it's like to be alone? To not have anyone?"

"I do," he told her. But she'd already turned away.

A tear slipped down her cheek as she watched her brother smash his head into the glass wall. It didn't so much as crack it. "I just found him," she whispered. Tearing her eyes from the screen, she looked at Hawke. "I just found you. And I'm not going to give up either of you without a fight."

The door opened and Kohl walked in. He quickly took in the scene in front of him. "Am I interrupting something?"

"No," Hawke answered as Everly walked around the desk and fell into one of the other chairs. He watched her for a moment before lifting his eyes to his friend. "No. We're just having a disagreement on how to deal with Matthew here." He pointed with his chin at the computer screen.

Eyes going back and forth between them, Kohl walked around the desk. "No change? Wait." He leaned in closer. "What the fuck?"

Hawke stood so he could have the chair. "It looks like they're getting somewhere with their experiments." Though he spoke to Kohl, his eyes were on Everly. He wanted to do something to comfort her. Hell, he wanted to do more than that.

The thought appeared: he could fight for her. And once

it was there, it wouldn't go away. If he didn't, she would go. Kohl would allow her to leave, eventually. He was sure of it. She was no help to them. Once they were sure her brother was out of the picture and Parasupe was taken down, he would let her leave. He might request she leave town. Maybe he would help her find her Thunder. But she would go.

I can fight for her. The only danger she posed was to herself. She would need someone with her to help her get through her first transitions.

Kohl waved his hand in front of his face. "Hey! You listening to me, man?"

His thoughts dispersed into little wisps of dreamlike smoke. But like smoke, the stench stuck and wouldn't be easily removed. "Sorry, what?"

"I was just saying, this is happening tomorrow night. Devon was in here most of the morning, and she thinks she got through the security. I'd like the coven prepared tonight. Everyone is in on this, other than a few essential vampires who will stay here and work the club like any other normal night. Dev's gonna work from here, too. When we get into position, she'll disarm the cameras and alarms remotely. Once we have the go ahead from her, we're taking these fuckers down."

Hawke glanced at Everly, but she was staring down at the desk, lost in thought. He turned his head away, just in case. "What about their prisoner?"

Kohl paused for a long time, and Hawke could feel his

hesitation. But when the order came, his voice didn't waver. "He goes down with the lab."

Even though he knew it had to happen, and he'd just been telling Everly the same thing, Hawke wished there was another way. For Everly's sake. "I'll take care of him."

Looking over the computer monitor, he met Everly's tear-filled eyes.

Then she got up and left the office, slamming the door behind her.

His first instinct was to go after her, but he knew he couldn't. She needed to deal with the reality of the situation. Hawke let his head fall back, then he took a calming breath before meeting Kohl's stare.

"You know what you have to do," Kohl told him. "I'll call Devon and have her keep an eye on Everly until we can decide what to do with her. I'll have Andrew stay with them, also." He paused. "I'm sorry it has to be like this, man. But I don't see any other way."

With a nod, Hawke said, "I'll go get the rest of the coven prepared for tomorrow."

CHAPTER 20

By some miracle, Everly made it out of the club without anyone stopping her. With the setting of the sun, people were starting to show up, and she pulled up the hood of the gray hoodie she'd grabbed from down in the caverns as she blended in with the crowd and made her way outside. Ducking low, she ran through the aisles of cars in the parking lot, searching for Hawke's vehicle.

She thought she saw it toward the back of the lot and clicked the key fob she'd stolen from his room after she'd sweet-talked the location from the bartender, Andrew. The headlights flashed, and she cursed under her breath, hoping no one had followed her outside yet. With a quick look over her shoulder toward the club, she ran for it, jumped into the driver's seat, and quickly locked the doors. Everly had no idea if that would keep out an angry vampire, but she figured it couldn't hurt.

Luckily, the car was a push button start, because her

hands were shaking so badly she didn't think she'd be able to get a key into the ignition. Her heart pounded a furious rhythm as she threw the car into drive, stomped down on the gas, and peeled out of the parking lot, checking the rearview mirror every few seconds to see if anyone was following her.

How fast could a vampire run?

Everly had no doubt Hawke would come after her. He thought he was saving her. She got that. But sometimes a girl didn't need saving. And sometimes she just needed to take care of shit her own damn self. Now, all she could do was hope she got to her brother before Hawke did, and hope he didn't catch her before she could. And hope he would forgive her once it was all over.

It's easier to ask for forgiveness than permission. She'd heard that somewhere. And if he didn't forgive her or she got herself killed, well, it was a chance she was willing to take. Matthew was her only blood relative. He at least deserved a chance. And Hawke wasn't willing to give him a chance at all.

Or her, for that matter.

A short time later, she pulled into the lot of her apartment building. Leaving Hawke's car in a guest spot, she ran upstairs and quickly grabbed what she needed. Trading keys for the rental she'd never returned and leaving his on the kitchen counter, she retrieved the gym bag she'd hidden in the back of her closet.

On the way out, Everly cracked open her apartment door and paused, checking things out before she left the safety of her home. The cat was on the table outside, watching her with his typical "I'm interested in what you're doing but too cool to show it" expression. No one else was around. She eased outside, pulling the door shut and locking it, and ran down to the rental car. She threw a quick thank you to the gods for the idea of getting it. An unrecognizable car was her only chance of getting anywhere near the Parasupe lab without being caught.

Everly didn't look back as she pulled out of the parking lot. She was afraid if she did, she would lose her nerve. Even though she'd been planning this day ever since she'd found out who had taken Matthew, she couldn't quite believe she was about to embark on a rescue mission to get her brother back. Or, why she would need to. Never in a million years would she have thought it was because he was one of those creatures who'd haunted her dreams. That *she* was one of those creatures.

But now that she knew, it didn't change a damn thing. He was still her brother, her only family. They could lean on each other for support. They could learn about their second natures together.

She had to pull over for a minute when she was within a few miles of the facility and pull up the map on her phone. Though she'd looked at it a million times, she didn't want to waste time taking a wrong turn and driving around aimlessly when Matthew's life was on the line. After confirming her location, Everly found the side road she'd been looking for and drove about three miles before pulling off into a small private drive. Driving forward until the car was out of sight of the road, she parked it in the grass and got out, taking her bag of supplies. She would walk the rest of the way.

The moon was in and out of the clouds tonight, and the threat of rain hung heavy in the cool air. After the fourth time Everly nearly stepped on a clump of cactus, she started shuffling her feet. Falling on to a group of those prickly bastards was not something she ever wanted to experience. When she could see the lights of the facility, she stopped and pulled a lab coat and a badge out of her bag. The coat was from a Halloween costume, and the badge was the one her contact had made for her. She was pretty confident it would pass inspection, as long as no one looked too closely. She'd had her guy copy the design from online photos of Parasupe employees, taken just a few weeks ago when they'd had a news conference about all the new ways they planned to save the human race from "climate change." She donned the coat, pulled her hair up into a tight twist on the back of her head and secured it with a few bobby pins, then clipped the badge to her jacket.

Now she just had to lie her way in. And this is where her deafness might actually come in handy.

Tucking a few things into her pockets, she stashed her bag behind a scraggly tree and approached the gate on foot. Armed guards huddled together to one side of the gate near the small shelter building, but they jumped to attention when they saw Everly, weapons at the ready.

She stopped and bent over with her hands on her knees like she was out of breath, then straightened and gave them a tired wave. As she approached, they eyed her clothing beneath her lab coat suspiciously, and Everly felt a twinge of nerves. She'd had no time to put on more scientist-like clothes. The mistake made her hesitate, but only for a step. Assuming an air of confidence she didn't feel, she ignored their looks and continued toward them.

One hand on her side and a smile of relief on her face, she gestured for them to open the gate. The guy on the left, big and bald with nasty teeth, asked her who the hell she was. Everly decided to call him Asshole number one. Pointing out her hearing aid, she signed the words, "I'm sorry. I can't hear you. Do you sign?"

Asshole number one looked at Asshole number two. He was almost the exact replica of Asshole number one, only with darker skin and better teeth, but with the same insolent stare. Asshole number two shrugged.

Everly signed, "Hey, asshole. Let me in so I can break my brother out."

Still, no signs of comprehension. She turned to the third guard, a younger guy who was side-eyeing his two friends and signed the same thing to him.

He shook his head as he shrugged and said, "I'm sorry, lady. I don't know what you're trying to tell us."

Rolling her eyes and sighing heavily, she gestured like she was writing on paper.

The three looked at each other, until finally the younger guy went inside the smaller building and looked around. He came back empty handed. "How can we not have any paper in there?"

"Because we used up the notepad and they just came and got the trash today," Asshole number two told him.

The younger one turned to her. "I have a pen?" He held it out.

Everly gave him her best *"what the hell am I supposed to do with that with no paper?"* look. Pulling out her phone, she pulled up her text messages and typed out, "I'm late, you idiots. My car broke down. Open the damn gate before I call Dr. Murphy and tell him you're holding up his experiment because the only doctor who knows how to do it is being held at the gate." Then she held it up in front of the young one's face. Everly had no idea if there was actually a Dr. Murphy, but she hoped they wouldn't know, either.

Either she lucked out and her made up doctor was real and a complete tyrant, or the doctors who worked there were harsh in general, because he turned to his companions and told the one closest to the door to go in and open the gate.

He gave them both a distrustful look, but ultimately went in and did what he was told.

Everly touched her fingers to her chin and signed, *"Thank* you." Heart pounding, she hurried through the gate and toward the largest building, hoping she was going the right way so as not to raise any more suspicion.

Now came the hard part. Convincing a few simple guards was easy enough, but if she ran into anyone who actually worked there it would be another matter altogether.

She found a side door to the large building, the word

"Laboratory" printed in gold letters right above a keypad to swipe her badge. Except her badge wouldn't work, of course, because it was fake.

Knowing there were cameras everywhere, she made a big scene of trying to get her badge to work, then threw up her arms and made her way around to the front. She spotted another way in and headed that way, only to get cut off when a doctor, or scientist, or whatever he was, came from the other side. Everly plastered a wide smile on her face as they met at the door, hoping he would do the gentlemanly thing and let her in. He did, after giving her a sweeping look that widened at her purple sneakers and got stuck at her boobs. With another smile she thanked him and hurried on her way. Which, hopefully, was a different direction than the one he was going.

Turned out it wasn't, and he followed her around the corner and rushed forward to open another door for her.

Everly smiled her thanks and stepped through, wondering if she should say something or if he'd noticed her aids, when the entire building rumbled beneath their feet. She stumbled into the man and he caught her by the elbow as they both regained their footing.

She looked up at him just in time to catch him saying, "…the hell was that?"

Everly shook her head when it happened again.

The doctor/scientist took off at a jog, and Everly followed him. She would rather have gone off on her own, but every door they'd passed had some kind of security measure on it. She wouldn't get very far without a badge that worked. Or without the correct fingerprints, she soon found out as they reached the center of the building.

Catching the heavy door, she followed him into a room and ran smack into his back. Her companion had pulled up short two steps inside the doorway, and Everly sidestepped to see what it was that had him in such a state. Her breath froze in her chest.

She recognized this place. It was the lab Devon had hacked into. Only it wasn't her brother she was looking at in horror. A full-grown dragon crouched inside some type of cell, one large wing half in and half out of the interior glass. Shattered pieces littered the floor, glinting in the flash of the emergency lights. Its skin was scaly green with patches of white that didn't look right, like maybe it was sick or something. Golden eyes burning with rage skittered about the room, glaring at the man before they found her and stuck. As she watched, it opened its mouth and inhaled, its chest filling with air, before releasing a stream of flames that would've burned her and her companion alive if it weren't for the glass along the front of the cage that was still intact. It yanked its wing back inside and then busted it through again, enlarging the hole it had already made.

Matthew had just tried to burn her alive.

Once the initial shock began to wear off, Everly had no doubt this creature was her brother. She could tell by the cock of its head and the color of its eyes and the feel of its rage. It was all very familiar to her. This creature that was her brother, and yet wasn't. The Matthew she'd gotten to know these last few months was a gentle soul with an easy smile and laughing eyes, not this raging beast. But something inside of her recognized her connection with him all the same.

Out of the corner of her eye, she saw a woman in a lab coat she hadn't noticed before. She was gesturing madly as she talked to the man Everly had followed there. Neither of them paid her any mind as she walked closer to the cage.

The dragon watched her, lowering its head as she gripped the bars surrounding it. Everly smiled, a strange sense of calm floating through her. "Think you can get yourself out of here?"

In response, he rammed the glass with his head, hard enough to shake the room, and then he threw back his head and opened his mouth wide. Long, white teeth nearly the length of her forearm glinted in the flickering lights.

She didn't need to hear the sound that came out, she could feel it reverberating all the way through to her bones. Losing interest in her, the dragon went back to working on the hole it had created and started ramming the points of an already bloody wing at the loose edges. Everly turned to check on the doctors and found them frantically shouting at each other as the woman stared at the computer screen in front of her and gestured with her hands as the man yanked at the door. Probably to let in the armed guards she was positive had been called to control the situation, given the flashing red alarm lights that were going off above the door.

Spotting a large microscope on a table to the side of the cage, Everly grabbed it. It was pretty heavy. Heavy enough to break glass.

CHAPTER 21

Hawke winced as the screech of a dragon ripped through his sensitive eardrums. Gritting his teeth, ignoring the taste of his own blood when his fangs sliced through the inside of his mouth, he ripped the entry gate to the Parasupe labs from its locking mechanism and entered the compound. Stealth wasn't necessary this time. No guards were there to stop him. By the sounds of it, they were otherwise occupied.

He'd come alone. There was no reason to ask Kohl to leave the coven when he could easily catch up to Everly and bring her back. But she'd manage to send him on quite a chase, and when he'd found the rental car parked down the road, he'd figured out how.

Had she planned this all along? And didn't tell him?

As he neared the lab at the center of the grounds, he fell into step with the fifty or so humans who had come running from other buildings. Some guards, some just humans in white coats who were working late. None of them paid the vampire in the hot pink shirt more than a passing glance. They had bigger things to worry about. Way bigger things.

Inside, the building shuddered around them, and some of the humans stopped and looked at each other while a few others wasted no time in turning around and hightailing it back outside. Even a few of the guards. Cowards. Hawke ignored them all, shoving bodies out of his way as he jogged toward the center of the building where they were holding Everly's brother. She was in there. And he didn't need the abandoned car to tell him that. Her blood called to him as soon as he'd gotten within a few miles of the place, long before he'd found the rental.

Guards were trying to bust in the door when he reached the interior of the lab. The building shuddered again, and he heard glass shattering and a woman screaming. Fear shot through him for a split second. But, wait. Not Everly. Someone else.

With little effort, he tossed bodies away from the door and ripped it from its hinges. As soon as it was gone, two humans in lab coats ran past him. Hawke let them go. He had little interest in them or the destruction of their lab. Which was exactly what was happening. Inside, Everly's shifter brother was in full dragon form, and using one wing to bust through the special glass between bouts of angry shrieks and gusts of fire.

Another woman with bright red hair in a lab coat was

near the hole the dragon was breaking. She wasn't trying to stop it. She was helping him break out.

"Everly! Stop!" She didn't hear him, of course. But she must've noticed something, felt something, because she stopped mid-swing and looked right at him. Hawke held his hands out in front of him, palms out. "Honey, please. Stop. You can't let him out of there." Pointing to the dragon, he shook his head to emphasize what he was saying.

She gave him a sad smile and went back to breaking glass without bothering to answer him. She wasn't nearly as effective as the dragon was, even with only one bloody wing, but that didn't matter. Judging by the size of that hole, Hawke knew he only had a matter of a minute or two before the dragon broke free.

Repetitive popping noises broke out around him before he could get to her, and he felt the red-hot heat of newly fired bullets streak by him as the guards finally shut their gaping jaws and started doing something about the situation.

By firing at bulletproof glass.

Without thought, Hawke launched himself at Everly and knocked her down onto the floor. Fire slammed into his chest, shoulder, and neck as some of the bullets found him. Bullets that would've went through Everly. The rest of them bounced off the glass or peppered the walls.

Rage flared inside of Hawke, burning so hot he wouldn't have been surprised if fire started shooting from his mouth like the dragon. These idiots were acting on panic, shooting everywhere, without a care that others might get hurt. He gave Everly a push between her shoulder blades to tell her to stay down, and then he rose up with a roar and rushed the nearest guard. Another wave of bullets pelted his side before he grabbed the gun and flung it so hard into the wall it broke into pieces and slid to the floor.

The human yanked a handgun from his waist, but before he could fire it, Hawke reached out with one hand and secured his wrist. Twisting it down and back bones splintered and popped as he sank his fangs into his neck. The gun slid from the human's hand.

He was on the other three before they saw him coming, all of their attention on the beast in the cell. Once he had them disarmed and either dead or unconscious, he turned to get Everly and get her the hell out of there.

And saw he was too late.

Everly had gotten under one of the metal tables along the side of the wall after the shooting had broken out. She curled up into the corner as the dragon, with one last, furious charge, broke through the glass and rammed into the cell bars. Two of them bent under the pressure of its weight. The dragon backed up, his sides inflating on a deep inhale.

"Everly!" Hawke's shout was lost in the flames as it heated the bars, then charged them again. A surge of relief made him lightheaded when he saw her still in the corner and apparently unharmed.

The dragon backed off again, preparing to send another round of fire.

Hawke moved fast. He knew he stood no chance against

the shifter. It would burn him alive with hardly a thought. His only chance was to get Everly the hell out of there and either wait it out until her brother changed back or call Kohl.

Appearing in front of her, Hawke dragged her from under the table and lifted her into his arms, preparing to run. But as soon as he turned around, he found himself impaled by a pair of crazed reptilian eyes. The dragon looked at Hawke, and then to the woman struggling in his arms.

"Motherfucker." He tightened his hold on Everly, and then he ran like he'd never run before, a trail of fire heating his back as he escaped the room and took off down the corridor.

"Let me down!" Everly twisted in his arms, trying to break his hold, but Hawke only held her tighter until they got outside. Emergency lighting flickered and dimmed, before it surged bright again, lighting up the grounds and destroying his hope of hiding in the shadows of the night.

Setting her on her feet, he grabbed her by the shoulders and shook her until she looked at him. "You cannot go back in there!"

Her eyes widened, and he saw a trace of fear in the gray depths that sent a spear of guilt through him. Hawke could only imagine what he looked like, all vamped out and bloody with the death of at least two of the guards on his hands.

"Everly—"

Her eyes fell to his throat. "Were you shot?" she asked.

Her shaking hands pulled at his shirt, buttons popping everywhere as she separated the material to see the flesh beneath. "Hawke! You're shot!"

The building behind her rocked on its foundation, and a few bricks fell to the ground.

"Mother*fucker*," Hawke muttered again as he watched it.

Everly spun around to see.

Hawke grabbed her arm and began to pull her away. He hadn't made it two steps when he stuttered to a halt and swayed on his feet. He was losing too much blood too fast before his body had a chance to heal itself. He needed to feed, but other than Everly, there was no one around to fulfill that need, and he couldn't take from her when she would need all of her strength to escape this place. The humans had fled the scene. Hawke couldn't blame them. He had no desire to be burned alive, either.

He realized Everly was holding him up. Hawke took her face between his hands and tried to focus on her. "Run."

She shook her head. "No. I'm not leaving you." Her jaw tightened. "Or him. That's my brother."

"That's not your brother right now, honey." He took a ragged breath. "You have to run. Get the hell out of here before he kills us both. Fucking run, Everly!" He shouted the words right in her face.

Tears filled her eyes, but she stood her ground. "No!"

Fuck. Hawke dropped his head, too exhausted to argue with her. He'd have to get her out of there himself.

Everly grabbed his arms and shook him. "Hawke!"

He raised his head, but she was looking behind him. Not

wanting to see, but knowing he needed to, Hawke twisted around.

The building was collapsing, piece by piece, as the dragon fought its way out. Its shrieks of rage filled the air, the roar of flames following each one busting out windows, black smoke billowing into the sky. As they watched, something exploded, the back half of the building began to crumble, and the dragon came bursting out of the thick cloud of smoke. It stretched its wings wide, blood dripping from the injured one, then gave them a hard flap, and rose high above the smoke as it released another shriek. This time of freedom.

Hawke realized they were standing out in the open and began edging his way over to the side of the closest building, one eye on the beast as he pushed Everly in front of him. For once, she didn't resist, stumbling backwards as she stared in awe at the creature hovering in the air above them.

"He's beautiful," she whispered.

Dragging her into the shadows, Hawke pressed her back against the wall, protecting her with his body, and grabbed her face to get her attention. "He's not in his right mind, Everly. Not even for a dragon. He won't know you."

She opened her mouth to speak, but before she could say anything, Hawke heard an ominous clicking sound and a rush of hot air. Before he could react, nerve endings screamed and then went dead as fire licked along his back. An involuntary roar of pain and anger ripped from his throat.

As his body slammed into Everly's, Hawke wondered if

this was how he was going to go out. If, after all the years he'd been alive and all the things he'd survived, this was the end. And the only regret he had was that he hadn't had time to make things right with this amazing female. She'd probably be better off. Hell, he couldn't even fucking protect her properly.

Suddenly, he was flat on the ground on his back and Everly was on top of him, swatting at the flames on his shoulders and sides with her bare hands before ripping off her lab coat and covering him with it. A second stream of dragon's fire seared the top of her head. The smell of burnt hair filled his nostrils. When it stopped, she sat up, and her own fire burned behind her eyes.

"I think I love you," Hawke whispered, knowing she wouldn't hear him, but needing to say it before death took him.

Everly stilled on top of him. Tears dropped from her chin to his face. And then she rose to her feet and was standing over him, staring up at her brother, screaming words Hawke couldn't comprehend through the rush of blood in his ears.

Smoke drifted around her, blurring his vision. Or, maybe it was his body shutting down. Vampires could take a lot of pain. He knew that firsthand. Over the long years of his life, Hawke had been chopped into with swords and axes. He'd been strung up from a tree with rope so coarse it cut into his throat before they even pulled it taut. And he'd taken more bullets than this night a few times over. None of it was pleasant; however, he always healed within hours.

But this time felt different. He had no way of knowing how deep the fire had burned through him, but it was possible it had burned through to his heart. And if that were the case, he may not heal this time.

Everly's form flickered above him. Her tears fell cold upon his face and neck. Or was that rain? She was still screaming, fist raised and red curls blowing in the wind.

There was a flash of light as she bent over Hawke, voice leaving her mid-scream, her body disjointed, bones breaking through skin that rippled with shades of red.

And then there was nothing.

CHAPTER 22

Everly watched Hawke's features contort in pain. His hand reached for her, lifting only a few inches before it fell back to the ground.

"Hawke?" Mesmerized by the sight of Matthew, she hadn't realized what he was about to do until fire shot from his mouth, straight at her and Hawke. Jostled from her frozen state of shock by Hawke's roar of pain, she threw herself forward, knocking him to the ground with a strength she didn't know she possessed, and following him down to smother the flames. She tried to remember what Hawke had said offhandedly that day about how much damage a vampire could take to his body before he wouldn't heal anymore. Remove his heart or his head, he'd said. So, would he heal from burns like this?

His eyes, dull and lifeless, searched her face. His mouth opened and closed, and then his dry lips formed the words, "I think I love you."

Sitting up, she stared down at him. "What?" Tears blurred her vision.

Matthew dipped into her line of vision, hovered for a moment, and then landed heavily not twenty feet in front of her, making the ground shake beneath them. She rose unsteadily to her feet, one foot on either side of Hawke's prone body, and began to scream at her only flesh and blood, words tumbling over each other as they were torn from her throat. She had no idea what she was saying, only that she hurt more than she had ever hurt before in her life. And it was *his* fault. This brother she'd spent years of her life searching for. She raged her pain at him until her throat burned, until the muscles in her body screamed with her. She didn't care if he wasn't himself. Didn't care if he couldn't understand her. All she cared about was that he had hurt this male.

This male that she also was beginning to love. This male who she'd felt an instant connection with. This male who had somehow crawled inside of her heart.

Searing pain shot hard and fast down her spine, bending her body at an impossible angle and cutting off her tirade mid-shout. Her head swam as she felt her bones shifting beneath the muscle. With an uncontrollable shudder, they cracked, then broke, tearing through her flesh and jerking her body around like a disjointed puppet. Streaks of fire ripped through her as the skin covering her shoulder blades split and tore. Turning her head to the side, she watched in horror as a skeletal wing stretched outward from her back.

Holy mother of God. She was shifting.

Everly screamed over and over as her body took over the transition, and when it was finished, she stood over a prone body, sucking in a lungful of cool, night air. Lowering her nose, she breathed in the male's scent.

Instinct made her step carefully so as not to crush the motionless form below her as she kept a careful eye on the other dragon. There was a sense of kinship to it, but it was quickly overridden by the recognition of a threat and a driving need to protect the male beneath her.

Spreading her wings wide, she prepared to defend her injured mate.

HAWKE DRIFTED in and out of a foggy sense of awareness. Or perhaps he was chasing the oblivion of death, and this was his mind's last hoorah.

But he couldn't be dying. Because only being alive hurt this fucking much.

The screech of a dragon above him jostled his consciousness.

Everly. Where the fuck was Everly?

Fighting the darkness that threatened to consume him, he pried his dry eyes open with sheer force of will. His back, from his neck to his thighs, screamed in agony. When he tried to sit up, he found he was stuck to the grass gripped in his fists. Gearing up to try again, he inhaled, and smelled the coppery scent of blood. *His* blood, if he were to take a guess. His body, with its advanced healing, was reacting to the inflammation already happening by sending fluids to the burned area, which in turn were leaking all over the ground below him.

Another shriek sounded, this time directly above him. He recognized her voice at once. Forcing his eyes open wider, he searched the sky above him for some sign of what was happening. Only there was something wrong. Instead of a blanket of stars, he found himself staring at a pattern of milky white scales tinged with red on the edges.

The scales shifted, sliding in and out of each other, and the ground trembled beside him. Letting his head fall to the side, he followed the pattern down to a large, clawed foot. Same on the other side. Following the sea of colorful scales down the length of his body, he found they darkened as they neared the tail. His mind, hazy in its efforts to protect him from his physical trauma, slowly grasped that this wasn't the dragon Parasupe had captured.

This was Everly.

She had shifted and was now standing over him like a predator protecting its hard-won meal. It was a situation he rarely, if ever, had found himself in before, normally being the one at the top of the food chain.

He needed to move, before he was stomped on. Or worse, covered in fire ants. One of the "perks" of living in Texas—even the ants tried to eat you. Hawke clenched his jaw to keep from making any noise as he tightened his abs and tore his raw back from the grass, rolling over onto his stomach. He didn't know if shifting would affect her hearing loss or not, but he also had a good guess as to who she was protecting her meal from. However, he underestimated what was left of his own strength and bumped into one of the talons. Instinctively, he froze.

Everly's large head swooped down. She huffed out a breath and then tilted it to the side to stare at him with one silvery eye. Recognition shimmered within it, and she sniffed his hair, inhaling deeply. Then she stepped forward, a low growl rumbling down the length of her throat above him.

She wasn't going to eat him. At least for now. She was protecting him. From her brother.

Fear shot through him. But not for himself this time. This time it was for her. Whether she planned to roast and eat him when this was all over was a moot point right now. This was her first shift, and she was going head to head with a dragon who couldn't be in his right mind, who had just tried to flambé them both. Sister or not.

Another explosion took out more of the building behind them and sent flames shooting into the air, lighting the area as bright as midday. Raindrops began to drip here and there from the sky, sizzling as they hit the fires. Taking advantage of the distraction, Everly advanced on her brother, leaving Hawke lying in the grass behind her. He took a steadying breath, then he gathered his arms and legs beneath him and pushed himself up onto all fours. The edges of his burned clothes tore at his inflamed skin and raw muscle. He felt the pain that rippled down his spine, and yet it didn't feel like pain at all, and he thanked the gods for destroyed nerve endings. Though he knew it was gonna hurt like a bitch when they started to grow back.

He stayed as he was for a few seconds. When he thought he could handle it, he pushed himself to his feet. The rain and cool night air felt good on his heated skin. He wasn't worried about infection, but he would need to feed if he was going to survive this. And soon.

Injured and weak, his first instinct was to get the hell out of there, but he couldn't leave Everly. She was young and inexperienced in her new form. There was no way she was going to win this fight. He needed to help her.

Before he could figure out exactly how he was going to do that, she spread her wings wide and flew up through the smoky air. With a glance at Hawke, Matthew followed her. Like a phoenix rising with her dark, red scales and majestic form, she went right for her brother, talons at the ready. They collided mid-air, the force of her charge sending them rolling over each other until they went crashing to the ground on the other side of the burning building. A shriek of rage preceded a fountain of fire that rose straight up from the ground.

Everly appeared high in the air. Tucking her wings, she swooped low, circling around Hawke, one eye fixed on him, before she again charged her brother who had joined her in the sky. They collided again, only this time she caught him in her talons and hung on.

She flapped her wings, dragging him up into the sky, rising higher and higher until they disappeared from sight.

Hawke wiped rain from his face and made his way over

to the shelter of the nearest building, only one story but it had a bit of a ledge around the roofline, enough to provide him some cover. Pulling his cell phone from his pocket, he wasn't surprised to see the screen cracked and the cover melted through to the battery. With a curse, he threw it to the ground.

He needed Kohl. But he had no idea what would happen if there were three dragons all fighting for dominance. Or if he would know enough not to hurt Everly. As far as Hawke knew, Kohl had never been around another dragon before while shifted, so there was no way to know.

A flash of lightning had him lifting his eyes to the sky, where the two dragons, necks and wings tangled, came spiraling down toward the ground. Hawke watched in horror as Everly crashed down hard, her brother atop her. The back of her head bounced off the ground and rolled on her neck. Her beautiful silver eyes blinked a few times, then slid closed.

She didn't move as Matthew wriggled around, and his heart stilled in his chest. For a moment, he couldn't move. But then he saw her chest rise and fall with breath as Matthew freed his wing and rose off her. Hawke looked around for a weapon. The burning building caught his eye, and although he really didn't want to go anywhere near any kind of flame ever again in his life, he kept one eye on the dragons as he limped over, looking for a brick, a piece of broken furniture, anything he could use. A large piece of what looked to be a desk or table that had been flung from the debris caught his eye, and he snapped off one of the legs.

Turning, he found himself pinned to the spot by Matthew's hateful glare. Hawke froze, makeshift weapon at the ready, in case he charged.

Everly stirred, drawing her brother's attention. Seeing him there, she quickly struggled to her feet, using the tips of her wings to help her, and the fight was on.

Only someone completely out of their mind would get in the middle of a battle between two beasts nearly the size of a two-story building, but Hawke couldn't just stand there and allow Everly to take on the weight of what she was trying to do. And there was no fucking way in hell he was gonna stand there and watch her get killed. So he waited, biding his time until the right moment.

With a smooth twist of her body, she ducked her head and came back up and around, clamping down on her brother's neck. She gave it a vicious shake, but he tore free, and they both took a few steps back, eyeing each other for the next attack.

Hawke dug down deep for the courage he would need for what he was about to do. Hefting the table leg like a spear, shivering violently from the wind and rain blowing against his burns, he saw his chance and ran straight toward the dragons. His muscles screamed. His vision went in and out. But he kept going, teeth clenched, fangs bared in agony and determination.

The dragon dropped its gaze from Everly and raised its head when it noticed him coming, then stepped away from her, turning to face this new threat.

Hawke didn't slow down, didn't give himself time to

think. Out of the corner of his eye, he saw Everly finally notice the crazy vampire running toward them. He knew he was taking a risk. He may have totally misread her earlier behavior. She might roast him alive as he passed and get back to her dragon match without a second thought. At least not until she reverted back to her human form.

With one last burst of energy, he pushed himself to go faster. Before either of them could react, he was beneath the male's head as it took a great inhale, preparing to finish what it had started.

With a scream of rage, Hawke swung his homemade spear up mid-stride, using his body's momentum to force the tip between the dragon's scales and straight into its heart.

The dragon staggered backward, large head swinging from side to side as it tried to dislodge the piece of wood.

Hawke fell on his ass. Struggling to get his legs back under him, he tried to keep Everly in his line of vision. His ankle twisted in a rut in the ground and he fell to his knees, catching himself on his hands. Black spots clouded his vision. His breath rasped through his lungs. He needed fluids. He needed blood.

He heard the sound of bone crushing bone. He heard Everly cry out, her voice an odd combination of a human scream and a dragon's screech, but he couldn't lift his head to see what was happening. Couldn't get his sorry ass off the ground to help her.

The wet ground rushed up at him, and everything went black.

CHAPTER 23

Everly lay on the cold, wet ground, breathing in the scent of the earth. Slowly and carefully, she pushed herself into a sitting position, her hair hanging in her face in a riot of damp, red curls. Light rain ran down her face and shoulders and she shivered, reaching automatically for her sweater, only to find she was nude.

Pushing her hair out of her face, she looked around, and then down at herself, trying to remember what had happened. Bruises covered her torso and legs, and she moved her body a bit, assessing her injuries. She appeared to have none that were serious.

To her left, the building that held the lab her brother was kept in was a nothing but a pile of smoking bricks. Turning her head to the right, she stared at the body lying there, feeling nothing but a strange numbness tingling through her body, starting at her hands and feet and working its way toward her center. Matthew lay there, as naked as she, with a large wooden post stabbed through the center of his chest. As Everly crawled toward him, she searched for any signs of life. But as soon as she got close enough to touch him, she realized it was too late. He was gone. His face slack and peaceful. She waited to feel sorrow at his loss. Rage. Guilt. But she must've been in shock, for the only thing she felt was a sense of relief.

Out of the corner of her eye, she saw something move in the grass.

Hawke.

Clumsily, she got to her feet and turned in a circle, searching for him. Hawke lay facedown about twenty feet away, partially hidden by debris from the collapsed building. As she made her way toward him, she saw his clothes were burned away, and the exposed skin of his back and part of his ass was red and blackened and blistered in places.

Everly knew nothing about burns, but she knew this was bad. Very bad. She looked around for something to cover him with, to protect him from the rain, but found herself at a loss as to whether that would be better or worse, so she knelt down near his head, shielding him with her body, and carefully touched his hair.

His mouth opened as though he were in pain.

Her heart fluttered in her chest and her eyes immediately filled with tears. Angrily, she swiped them away. It seemed all she'd been doing the past twenty-four hours is cry. "Hawke?"

He moved again, and after a few tries, his eyes fluttered open, black as the night. They shot back and forth wildly for a moment before they focused on her bent leg, so close to his mouth. His upper lid pulled back and he flashed his fangs.

Without a thought to her own weakened state, Everly offered him her wrist.

To her surprise, he pulled back, rolling onto his side. "Help me up."

She managed to get him into a sitting position. Then she offered her wrist again.

But he shook his head. "We need to get out of here."

"You need to feed," she countered. "Please, Hawke. Take it. It's okay." She shoved it closer to his mouth.

Taking her arm in both hands, his mouth twisted into a snarl. He looked at her once more, and when she nodded, he sank his fangs deep.

Everly winced from the roughness of the bite, and then sucked in a breath as he took his first draught. Her body, numb with exhaustion and grief, woke up with a vengeance, flashes of dark heat shooting straight to her core. She moaned as he sucked at her vein with deep pulls. Dark eyes flashed open, locking on hers, and shivers ran up and down her spine, the air suddenly thick and hard to breathe.

Soon, he was sitting straighter and those eyes were roaming over her body. Everly felt everywhere they touched her, like embers burning away the chill of the rain with sweet heat. She felt the vibration of his growl. Heart pounding, her breath caught. Her free hand touched his arm, his face, before dipping between her thighs to ease the ache there. His eyes burned as he watched her. But it wasn't what she wanted. She wanted Hawke. So she contented herself with the feel of his strong thigh beneath her fingers and waited for him to finish.

As she watched him feed, a flush of guilt heated her cheeks and chest. He was injured. Her brother was dead. And here she was thinking about nothing but sex.

With one last pull, Hawke withdrew his fangs and licked her wound closed before pressing a fervent kiss on the sensitive skin. Releasing her wrist, he took her face between his hands and pulled her in for a kiss. "Thank you," he told her, and then pulled her to him again.

Everly returned his kisses with wild abandon, rising to her knees to get closer to him before she remembered and lurched away.

Hawke cupped her cheek. "What is it? What's wrong? Did I hurt you?"

She shook her head. "No. No, of course not. It's just..." The words tumbled over each other on her tongue, so finally, she just waved her hands around, taking in every-thing around them. Where they were. The rain. Her lack of clothes. Her brother. Him.

As though he were snapping out of a trance, Hawke jumped to his feet, bringing her with him. She barely caught a, "What the fuck..." before she lost sight of his mouth. She spun around, terrified someone had caught them. Someone from Parasupe.

But Hawke gripped her arm to get her attention and shook his head. "No one is here. Not yet. But you're right, honey. We need to get the hell out of here. Gods! I wasn't fucking *thinking*." He kissed her again, fast and hard. Then he left her shivering in the rain as he retrieved her lab coat and brought it to her. It was wet, and it had a few burn holes, but at least it covered her.

As she pulled it closed and buttoned it up with shaking hands, she turned to ask Hawke about Matthew, but Hawke wasn't with her. He was over by her brother. She watched as he carefully pulled the large piece of wood from her brother's chest, and then lifted him into his arms.

Silently, her heart in her throat, she waited for him to join her, and then they walked out of that place.

Together.

The ride back to the caverns was silent. Hawke had taken off what was left of his shirt and laid it over Matthew in the back seat. Every few seconds, Everly saw him checking the rearview mirror, but no one followed them. She assumed most of the guards had gotten blown up in the explosions. The ones who weren't in the building had taken off and probably wouldn't have a job come tomorrow.

They arrived back at the caverns with about forty-five minutes to spare before the sun came up. Gathering her brother's body from the back seat, Hawke took him around the back of The Caves, then went into the little storage shed the groundskeepers used and returned with a shovel. Everly picked out a nice spot, and Hawke got to work. Together, they buried him. Then Hawke gave her a few minutes alone, though he didn't go far.

Everly stood in front of her brother's grave. She wasn't used to this sort of thing, and she didn't know what to say.

"I'm so sorry, Matthew. For everything." Then she just stood there silently, thinking of the years they'd missed out on, and the ones they could've had. She didn't cry. She just felt…hollow.

Hawke touched the back of her elbow. "We need to get inside," he told her.

Everly nodded, noting the sun's rays just beginning to lighten the edge of the horizon with orange. She realized she was freezing and immediately felt bad for making Hawke stand outside with no shirt on. With one last look at the fresh mound of dirt, she followed him into The Caves.

He escorted her to her new room and watched as she went inside and turned on the light by the bed. Now that they were back, she expected him to leave right away as he always did. Her brother was gone and no longer a threat. She fully expected to be next, one way or another.

But he didn't leave. Instead, he followed her inside and shut the door. When she looked up, she found him standing there, staring.

"How is your back?" she asked. "I can look at it if you want. Do you need more blood? Or…or…" She came to a stuttering halt. Tears filled her eyes for the eight-hundredth time that night. "I killed him. Didn't I?" Her knees gave out and she sank onto the bed.

Hawke moved then, rushing over only to stand awkwardly in front of her. After a moment, he kneeled so their eyes were level with each other. Placing his hands on either side of her hips, he was careful not to touch her. And that made her feel even worse.

"No," he said. "You did not kill your brother." His chin lifted. "I killed him. I had to, honey. There was no other choice. You were hurt, and I had to."

She saw the words, but it took a few seconds for them to penetrate. "You killed my brother." The words felt thick on her tongue. "You."

Hawke sat back on his heels, his face expressionless, but his eyes held hers, begging for understanding. "Yes."

She thought that over. "I'm not sure how I feel about this." Her hands felt like ice and she tucked them between her thighs. "I'm not sure how I *should* feel about this." She searched his face, looking for malice or satisfaction or something that would make it easy on her. But there was none of that. Only a deep sorrow around his dark eyes, and conviction to the set of his jaw that he'd done what he believed was right.

His bare chest rose and fell. "You can hate me if it will make it easier on you," he told her. "But it had to happen, Everly. He was too far gone. And I couldn't let you be the one responsible. I couldn't let you live with that." He paused. "More than any of that, I couldn't stand there and allow him to hurt you, so I did what I felt I had to do."

"I don't really remember much except feeling *so much rage* when he came after you. After us. And then there was a lot of pain." She shrugged. "Then I woke up and it was all over."

"That's all you remember?"

She nodded.

"Would you like to know what happened?"

She did, but not right now. She couldn't handle anything else right now. "Not today," she said. "I just want to get a shower and go to sleep."

He pushed himself to his feet. "Yeah, sure. I'll go." Her heart lurched in her chest, but he didn't leave right away. "Everly, you saved me tonight. I just…I want you to know that. You were beautiful, and brave, and fearless. And you saved my life. Thank you."

With a gentle touch of his fingertips on her cheek, he turned and walked toward the door, and she saw the angry wounds on his back. Everly stood and caught his hand before he could go. "I wish you would let me help you with your burns."

His eyes closed for a brief moment before he smiled at her. "It'll heal, thanks to you. I just need a shower."

"You can shower here," she offered. The words had flown from her mouth without thought. Unsure where this need was coming from, she took a small step back, but she didn't release his hand. However, after evaluating things, she stepped closer again. She needed him tonight. She needed him always.

Hawke gently pulled his hand from hers. "Everly—"

She stopped him before he could say it. "I know. We're not supposed to be together. Dragons and vampires don't mix and blah, blah, bullshit." Everly looked down at her bare feet and his muddy shoes. Then she raised her chin. "If you feel anything for me at all, please stay with me tonight. Just for tonight. And whatever happens tomorrow happens."

His mouth twisted in disgust. But not for her. For

himself. "How can you ask me this knowing I just killed your only family?"

She gave him a small smile. "You're an honorable male, Hawke. He was my brother, yes. But he was also dangerous. He tried to kill you. He tried to kill *me*. Twice." She held up two fingers, then paused, hating to admit this part but knowing it was true. "And he was beyond help. I know that now. It wasn't his fault, but it was true. Much as I wish it could've been different. I may have saved you tonight, but you saved me, too. If you hadn't shown up, my stupid ass would probably have burned with the lab."

Taking her face between his hands, his eyes searched her own in disbelief. "Can you forgive me, Everly? Maybe not right now. But someday?"

"Yeah. I can." And she realized it was completely true. "Someday." She covered his hands with hers. "So, stay with me."

CHAPTER 24

Hawke's chest tightened until he could barely breathe. "I would like that," he told Everly. "I would like that very much."

"I can see a 'but' coming." She stepped into his body, rising up on her toes until he felt her soft breasts against his chest, and he moaned. He couldn't help it. Her clear gray eyes searched his as her hands roamed up his arms, careful not to touch the back of his shoulders. "If this is my last night here, I want to spend it with you."

"No 'but'", he told her. And he was surprised that he meant it. Consumed by his hunger for her, her words didn't at first penetrate. And when they did, it was like a shot of ice to his rising libido. "Are you going somewhere?" He answered for her before she could say anything. "You can't leave." *Me,* he wanted to say. *You can't leave me.*

"I have a job I need to get back to, and an apartment, and

a cat. If Kohl doesn't send me away, I'll still have to leave eventually."

"The cat is yours?"

She rolled her eyes. "Well, he may as well be. We've bonded."

"What about your other half?"

Everly sighed and took a step back. She didn't go far, but the chasm between them may as well have been the size of an ocean. "I don't know what to do about that. And honestly, I'm a little scared." She wrinkled her nose. "No, that's a lie. I'm fucking terrified."

"Kohl can help you learn to deal with that side of your nature."

She laughed, the sound short and without humor. "I don't know about that. I get the feeling he doesn't like me very much."

Hawke shook his head and reached for hand, needing some kind of connection between them. "It's not that."

"Then what is it?"

"It's hard growing up with a foot in two different worlds. He just…never felt like he belonged anywhere. And he doesn't want to take the chance of another going through that."

"It doesn't have to be two different worlds," she said quietly.

Looking at her standing before him, with a smudge of dirt on her face and her red hair curling wildly around her face, Hawke believed that was true. It felt good to be around her. It felt right.

It felt like home.

He rubbed the dirt off her face with his thumb. "I'm beginning to believe you."

She started to say something, and then she stilled. "Hawke, what are you—"

Heart pounding in his ears, he cut off her words with a kiss. Just a brush of his mouth on hers, really. Everly moaned, her lips parting beneath his, and he sucked her full bottom lip into his mouth, biting gently until he tasted the sweet warmth of her blood.

When he released it, they were both breathing heavily. "Let's go get that shower."

Without another word, she led him to the bathroom.

Hawke watched as she turned on the water, appreciating the view of her strong calves and rounded thighs, then he helped her take off the wet lab coat and shed his shoes and pants and boxer briefs, shucking it all into the corner.

The hot water stung his back like a bitch when they got in. Hawke hissed with the pain, and quickly adjusted the temperature.

Turning so Everly was under the spray of water, he washed the remnants of the night's horrors from her body, memorizing every slope and curve. Every spot that made her flinch with laughter and sigh with longing. Then they switched positions so she could do the same.

When they were clean, he pressed her against the tiles and kissed her hard. His hands roamed over silky skin and soft curves, lingering on the sensitive spots as he ran his tongue and teeth down her throat to taste her hardened nipples. Pulling one into his mouth, he flicked the tip with tongue and then bit down as he found the wet heat between her soft thighs. Everly cried out, her fingers twisting in his hair to hold him at her breast, her hips bucking against his palm. He drank in her cries, her blood, her passion like a man starved, feeling all of it heal him physically and spiritually. And when she came, he lifted her leg around his hip and slid into her so he could feel her pulse around him.

He came fast and hard, his cries mingling with hers. And then he pressed his forehead to hers, still inside of her, and waited until his heartbeat slowed and he caught his breath. Then he turned her around and fell to his knees behind her. Gripping her hips, he pulled her toward him and found her sweet core with his tongue.

When the water began to cool, and her legs shook with the effort to hold herself up, he dried her off and took her to bed.

More than once, he looked into her eyes to find the dragon inside of her looking out at him. But Hawke just smiled, and the dragon would smile back as she arched her body into his caress.

Hawke had no idea what would happen when this day was over and they had to come back to reality, but he planned to make it a day neither of them would easily forget.

Eventually, they slept, and he woke to the sound of her stomach growling under his ear. Lifting his head from her torso, he blinked awake as he reached for his phone, then remembered it was melted.

Leaving Everly asleep, he found a pair of Kohl's jeans and slipped them on. They were a little long, but otherwise fit pretty well. In the bathroom, he checked out his injury in the mirror and was happy to see the burns were healing well, thanks to Everly.

It must be that dragon blood.

In any case, he was grateful.

A little while later, he came back to find Everly coming out of the bathroom, fully dressed in khaki pants and a white T-shirt with a shiny gold elephant on the front. Her hair, as usual, was down to cover her ears. She smiled wide when she saw him. "Hi."

"Hey." Hawke set down the paper bag he carried on the dresser and started taking out container after container of barbeque he'd picked up from the restaurant she'd taken him to.

"Oh my God, that smells wonderful. Thank you! I'm starving." Grabbing as much as she could carry, she settled cross-legged on the bed and dug in.

Hawke watched her with amusement, wondering where she put it all. After a few minutes, he went over to the chair and sat down. Touching her knee to drag her attention away from the food, he said, "We need to talk, Ev."

She studied him as she chewed, probably noticing a lot more about him than others who could hear normally did. Her eyes flicked down his body and back to his face. Picking up a napkin, she wiped her mouth as she swallowed. "I think this is the first time I've seen you in jeans and a T-shirt."

Hawke frowned, looking down at his borrowed clothes. "They're Kohl's."

"Ah." Another forkful of coleslaw went in her mouth, but little worry lines creased her brow. "Is this it?"

Confused, Hawke looked at the boxes of food. "Would you like more? I can run back to the restaurant."

She shook her head, her hair a riot of red curls around her face. "No, this is plenty. Thank you," she said again. Then she set her food on the nightstand. "I meant, is it time? Have you guys decided what you're going to do to me?"

He didn't miss the sarcastic tone. And he deserved it. She wasn't a problem to be handled. She was a smart, funny, courageous—and, at times, dangerous—female who deserved more respect than what she'd been shown. "We need to go talk to Kohl."

"And what are we going to say to him?"

Hawke took a curl between his thumb and forefinger and rubbed the soft strands between his fingers before pulling it straight and watching it bounce back again. He was nervous, more nervous than he'd been in…well, a very long time. "I was thinking that you and I need more time." He smiled. "To get to know each other."

"I thought vampires and dragons weren't allowed to mix and mingle?" Despite the teasing tone of her voice, her entire body was fraught with tension as she waited for his answer.

"I'm thinking, perhaps, that you were right. That rule is one that needs to be bent, or broken in two and thrown into the fire to burn."

He waited for her reaction, any reaction, but she just sat there, still as before. "Why?" she finally asked.

"Why?"

"Yeah. What changed your mind?"

Hawke scratched at his beard. It was a fair question. "Well, I find the thought of you walking out of here…" He searched for the words, something eloquent, and finally he just shrugged. Terrified she would leave, and terrified she wouldn't, he said, "I don't want you to go, Ev. I want you to stay here. With me. I can't guarantee it will work out, or that it will be easy. All I know is the thought of not hearing you laugh or kissing your lips or seeing what kind of crazy outfit you're going to wear next makes me fucking miserable. I *crave* you, Everly. All of you. Even when I'm sitting right in front of you."

"You're one to talk about the crazy outfits," she told him. Then she smiled. "I'm very happy that you finally pulled your head out of your ass."

Hawke laughed, taking both her hands in his. "I need to talk to Kohl."

"What are you going to say to him?"

"I'm going to tell him the truth."

"And what if he doesn't want to listen?"

Kissing her knuckles, he thought about that. "I don't know. I'll change his mind. Or, we'll both leave." As soon as the words left his mouth, he knew they were right. Everly belonged with him, and if his friend couldn't see that, Hawke was prepared to go with her. They could protect each other.

"Really?"

"Really."

She jumped from the bed with a little squeal and landed in his lap. Wrapping her arms around him, she hugged him tight.

Hawke hugged her back and breathed her in. He'd never felt anything so good as this female wrapped around him.

CHAPTER 25

Everly was nervous as she and Hawke went above ground to go meet Kohl at his lakefront property.

When they arrived, Kohl was pacing back and forth across the new drive, waiting for them. His eyes went from Hawke to Everly and back to Hawke, but he didn't say a word until they approached him.

"What the fuck happened last night?" Kohl immediately looked at Everly. He took a stop toward her, stopping only when Hawke stepped in his way. "What the fuck did you do?"

Rather than retreating, she stepped forward, closing the distance between them. "I saved his fucking life, that's what I did."

Both males stilled, regarding her warily.

She rubbed her face with her hands. That may have come out louder than she'd intended. "I'm sorry," she told Kohl. "I'm tired. And my brother is dead." The last word caught on a sob. She didn't try to hide her tears. Over the span of the day, in between fits of sleep, the cold reality of the night before seeped beneath her skin until even Hawke's embrace couldn't warm her.

"What happened?" Kohl asked again, quieter this time.

"Just what the lady said," Hawke replied. "She saved my life. Can we go inside, man? We need to talk."

Kohl rubbed the back of his neck. "Yeah, sure."

Inside the two-story house, she found the downstairs at least was almost finished. Though there were no windows, it was light and bright and open, lit up by numerous portable lamps.

A small card table and a set of four folding chairs were set up in one corner. Kohl moved some papers off of it, setting them on the floor, and indicated for them to sit. "I told the crew to take the night off. The rest of the coven will be here shortly." He glanced at Everly. "I'm sorry, I don't have anything to drink."

She showed him the water bottle in her hand. "I'm good. Thank you."

Pulling up a chair, he joined them at the table. "Are you both okay? I've been trying to fucking call you all day. I was about to head over to The Caves when you texted me."

Everly looked at Hawke, leaving it up to him as to how much he wanted to tell Kohl.

"Yeah. We're okay. But Parasupe's lab is in rough shape."

"What the fuck happened?"

Hawke told him everything, from the time he walked out of the office and realized Everly had taken off with his car, to the race against the sun as they drove back with Matthew's body. When he was finished, he reached over and grabbed Everly's hand beneath the table, then looked back at his coven Master. "Kohl, you and I need to talk."

Kohl frowned. "Is there something else?"

"We need to talk about Everly."

"And since this concerns my life, I think I should be in on it," she told him.

Kohl glanced back and forth between the two of them. Whatever he saw there, he didn't seem to be very happy about it. Leaning back in his chair, he rubbed the back of his neck. "You're right," he told her. "I apologize. I've been a bit of an asshole about all this, and you don't deserve that shit from me."

"Apology accepted," she told him with a smile. "I get it. Having the responsibility of the lives of an entire coven of vampires would get to anyone."

"Thank you," he told her.

"Kohl." Though he was speaking to him, Hawke was looking at Everly. "I want Everly to come and live with us. More specifically, I want her to come and live with *me*."

Kohl sat forward in his chair, and gave Hawke a hard stare. "Hawke, you know that isn't possible."

"This isn't the same situation as your parents, man. Everly is mine. If she leaves, I'm leaving with her."

Everly felt her heart swell until she didn't think it would fit in her chest. She realized this was the first time ever someone was fighting for her. That someone wanted to *keep* her.

Everly is mine.

The words sent a thrill through her, and an answering feeling of possessiveness toward him. "But I would like to stick around," she told Kohl. "I could really use your help dealing with all of this dragon stuff."

Kohl's body jerked backward on a laugh and he rolled his eyes. "I don't know how much help I'd be there. I'm still learning about this stuff myself." Looking back and forth between them, he got serious. "And if I don't agree to this? You're really gonna just leave your family? Leave me?"

Everly turned to Hawke, suddenly nervous. This was the true test.

But Hawke only squeezed her hand beneath the table and told him, "It's either that, or I will have to challenge you as Master of this coven."

Kohl sat back in his chair, the look of disbelief on his face almost comical. And Everly knew it had nothing to do with Kohl being a dragon and a lot to do with their relationship. "You're gonna fight me?"

"No. I won't have to."

"It's the law, Hawke. If you challenge me, it's a fight to the death."

But Hawke shook his head. "Not if it's a matter of lineage."

Kohl frowned.

Hawke pushed his hair back from his face. "I've never told you this before. Hell, I've never told anyone, except for Everly." His chest rose and fell on a deep breath. "Our previous Master was my half-brother. His blood runs in my veins. I can challenge your position without a fight. There are still some older vampires in the area who remember when I first came here, and they'll back me up. The coven will be mine to run as I choose." He glanced over at her and she smiled. "And I choose Everly." He turned back to his friend. "But I don't want to do that, and I really hope you don't force the issue. Any children that happen between you and Devon or Everly and I, it won't be the same as when you were born. Think about it, man. They'll grow up with us, in a family who cares about them. They'll be safe and protected."

"And a target for anyone who finds out about them," Kohl finished.

But Hawke shook his head. "They'll be safe. Hell, with a hybrid for a father or a dragon for a mother, anyone in their right mind would run in the other direction. Besides, who says we have to have kids?" Again, he ran his hand through his hair. "I don't want to challenge you, man. You know I've never wanted this. But I will if that's what it takes."

Kohl got up and walked away from the table. Everly could see his indecision, and she honestly couldn't blame him. Growing up in foster homes had left her with a similar sense of not belonging. And she'd learned to live with it. But now, she'd found her home, and she wanted to stay.

Getting up from the table, she went over to him. "I will understand your decision, Kohl, whatever it might be, and I respect where you're coming from. But I want you to know that I truly care about Hawke. I would never purposely hurt any of you. I just want to be with him. And I think you can understand that. What would you do if someone tried to come between you and Devon?"

His gaze clashed with hers, but he said not a word.

She shrugged. He didn't have her fooled. She'd seen the way he looked at her. "I just want to be with Hawke, that's all. I'm not trying to come between your friendship. I truly don't want that."

Kohl narrowed his eyes, and she was worried she'd taken things too far. But then he suddenly smiled. "I have a better idea." Striding back over to the table, he said something to Hawke.

As Everly approached, Hawke was looking at him like he'd lost his mind. "Two Masters?"

"Yes," Kohl told him as she retook her seat. "Why the hell not? If we're changing rules, who says we can't change that one, too? You're way better at this than me, Hawke. We both know it, and honestly, I'm really getting sick of saying it. The coven looks up to you, and they respect you. But they also want me, or rather, the dragon, to protect them."

Two Masters? They were going to co-Master the coven?

Hawke shook his head. "No. No way, man. It won't work."

"Why the hell not?"

"It just…won't. There can only be one Master."

Kohl threw up his hands and rolled his eyes. "Fine. It's yours. I concede. Everly here is my witness."

"You concede?" Hawke threw back his head and laughed. "You son of a bitch. You planned this all along, didn't you?"

Kohl grabbed his hand and they shook. "Nah, man. It just

came to me. But, seriously. We both know you're the right vampire for the job. It's in your blood. Quite fucking literally. And I never wanted this." He looked at Everly. "I only wanted Devon, and did what I had to do to protect her. Just like you're doing right now."

Hawke stared at Kohl, who stared back with one brow lifted in challenge. Then he scrubbed his face and looked over at Everly. His eyes softened. "Fine. I accept your forfeit."

Everly grinned at Hawke. "Does this mean I have to call you Master in bed?"

He gave her a naughty smile. "Only if you want to stay on my good side."

Kohl rolled his eyes again. With a wave, he left them alone as Hawke stood and took her into his arms.

"Let's go home," he said.

"Yes, Master."

Everly grinned as he flashed his fangs.

THANK you so much for reading the Southern Dragons! These characters appeared in my head out of the blue when my husband and I decided to stop at The Natural Bridge Caverns just north of San Antonio, TX. It was the weirdest thing, and I'm sure the rest of our group thought I was absolutely out of my mind when I whipped out my little notebook and started whispering (loudly) to my husband about dragons and vampires living underground. LOL

If you'd like to read more vampires, download A VAMPIRE BEWITCHED right now!

Book 1 is FREE to get you started into the series.

"Not since the early days of the Black Dagger Brotherhood have I so enjoyed a paranormal romance!" -Amazon UK

If shifters are more your style, download LONE WOLF'S CLAIM, book 1 of The Kincaid Werewolves.

"I completely fell in love with Brock, the werewolf with the heart of gold, that never stops fighting no matter what he is thrown up against... swoon...." Romance Authors That Rock

L.E. Wilson writes romance starring intense alpha males and the women who are fearless enough to tame them — for the most part anyway. ;) In her novels you'll find smoking hot scenes, a touch of suspense, some humor, a bit of gore, and multifaceted characters, all working together to combine her lifelong obsession with the paranormal and her love of romance.

Her writing career came about the usual way: on a dare from her loving husband. Little did she know just one casual suggestion would open a box of worms (or words as the case may be) that would forever change her life.

Lattes and music are a necessary part of her writing

process, though sometimes you'll find her typing away at her favorite Starbucks. She walks two miles to get there, to make up for all of those coffees.

On a Personal Note:

"I love to hear from my readers! Contact me anytime at le@lewilsonauthor.com."

Keep In Touch With L.E.
lewilsonauthor.com
le@lewilsonauthor.com

www.ingramcontent.com/pod-product-compliance
Lightning Source LLC
Chambersburg PA
CBHW021125190726
48288CB00008B/2511